LONDON'S BURNING

OTHER TEAM REAPER THRILLERS

LONDON'S BURNING

A TEAM REAPER THRILLER
BOOK 16

BRENT TOWNS

ROUGH
EDGES
PRESS

Rough Edges Press
An Imprint of Wolfpack Publishing
1707 E. Diana Street
Tampa, FL 33610

roughedgespress.com

Paperback ISBN 978-1-68549-527-5
Ebook ISBN 978-1-68549-526-8

LONDON'S BURNING

CHAPTER 1

LONDON, ENGLAND

BOB MURPHY PULLED his cap down farther as he crossed Tower Bridge in the small, enclosed lorry. Cars passed in the opposite direction, a steady stream making their way across the Thames toward Riverside. His heart skipped a beat as he passed a police car. Turning his face away, he looked down at his watch. Everything had to be perfect for it to work.

After getting off the bridge, he traveled down Mansell Street. From there, it was a matter of getting onto Aldgate, then following a rabbit warren of different streets and lanes until he reached Saint Mary Axe.

Murphy licked his dry lips for the tenth time as a thin bead of sweat broke out onto his brow. At a busy intersection, his mission almost ended when he tried to pull out in front of a cab. The cab driver blasted his horn at Murphy, and the Irishman from Belfast looked out his window and flipped his middle finger at the indignant driver, mouthing, "Fuck off."

He jammed the shift back into first, the gearbox grinding even with the clutch depressed, and grumbled, "Fucking cock," as the lorry lurched forward with a low growl.

He looked at his watch once more. He was on time despite the building traffic. Indicating his intention to turn right, he eased the lorry around the corner into yet another lane. Up ahead, he could see people milling around in the middle of the one-way thoroughfare.

Murphy slowed the lorry, his objective to avoid any incidents that might attract undue attention. The gathering, however, wasn't moving. The people just turned to stare at him.

The group consisted entirely of young men, some attired in hoodies, some with shaved heads. All wore jeans and had bandanas of some description around their arms to identify them. They appeared to be a small selection of the Leadenhall Mob, street thugs who haunted the back lanes where deals were done and battles were fought with anyone they took a dislike to. Having been previously warned about them, Murphy was glad that he'd come prepared but hoped his backup wouldn't be necessary.

Rolling the lorry to a stop, he wound down the window as a pair of young men broke away from the others and approached. His right hand slipped under his coat and wrapped around the butt of a Glock 19.

The duo looked cocky, full of themselves as they stared at the middle-aged man. The self-designated leader gave him the once-over before asking, "Where the fuck you think you're going, muvverfucker?"

He glanced at his friend and sniggered.

Murphy nodded at the end of the lane. "Me? I'm just going that way. Something to deliver."

The young man smiled wickedly. "What you know, a fucking Mick. You're not going anywhere, mate. Not along here, that's for sure."

Murphy said nothing.

"What you got in there anyway?" the leader asked, standing on tiptoes to peer past him into the cargo space.

"Nothing that would interest you, boyo."

"Boyo, is it?" came the retort. He glanced briefly at his partner, then back at Murphy, and fixed him with a malicious glare.

The look was an intimidation tactic designed to cow the driver, but it met with no success. Over the years, Murphy had seen a lot of bad shit, and dealing with these young punks didn't warrant a high number on that list. "Listen, *boyo*. I have a delivery to make, and you and your pals are holding it up. I'll ask you nicely: please move?"

The young man's stare hardened, and he produced a knife. The move was obviously a signal to his compatriots since they all appeared suddenly, armed with a variety of different blades: knives, machetes, a meat cleaver. Murphy shook his head. "Son, I hope your da smacked your mother in the mouth when you were born for giving birth to such a poor fucking excuse for a kid. Otherwise, you would have known not to bring a knife to a gunfight."

With one smooth movement, the Glock came clear and poked out the window of the lorry. It crashed once, and the young man took a round to the face. He collapsed onto the street in a bloody heap. Murphy changed his aim and shot the friend, this time in the throat. While the second guy was dying, the Irishman climbed out of the lorry and began shooting the remaining gang members, who had started to turn and flee.

He fired three more shots. All went wide, aimed to scare the gang members off.

Murphy muttered a curse and climbed back into the lorry, which was still idling. He engaged first gear and once more lurched forward, again looking down at his watch. He was three minutes behind schedule.

———

While Murphy was restarting his journey, two other lorries were nearing the end of theirs. Each was on approach to their target bridge, the first being Westminster, the other Waterloo. Coming to almost simultaneous halts, the drivers parked their vehicles crosswise, intended to create as much congestion as they could. The first part of their missions complete, the drivers settled in to wait.

The buildup of traffic in both directions didn't take long, and soon the two bridges became a mess of backed-up cars and honking horns. Still the drivers waited.

Five cars back from the parked lorry on Waterloo Bridge, Henry Myers climbed out of his vehicle and straightened, trying to work out what the hell was happening. He looked at the driver in the car ahead of him. "Oi, what the fuck is going on?"

The man shrugged. "Must be some sodding protest thing, mate. You know, like that cow who's always going on about the climate change."

"Not on this fucking bridge, mate," Henry growled and started forward. "Not today."

As he walked past the other driver, the man called to him, "What are you going to do?"

"Move this prick out of the way. I've got somewhere to be."

Henry made his way in between the vehicles until he reached the lorry. He walked up to the driver's side door and tried to open it, but the door was locked. He banged his fist on it, shouting, "Hey, knobhead. What do you think you're doing? Get moving. Some of us have to be places."

There was no reply or sign of movement.

Henry walked around to the front of the lorry, and with a bit of effort, pulled himself up onto the bumper. "Hey! What the—"

Gaining his balance, he leaned against the bonnet and stared in through the bug-splattered windshield. The driver was sitting there with his eyes closed as though he'd fallen asleep. In the man's left hand was something Henry couldn't quite identify. He did, however, have no trouble recognizing the wires running from the object, and he felt his bladder release.

"Sweet mother of God," he managed to gasp as the lorry, loaded with its nitrate bomb, exploded.

———

On Westminster Bridge, in sight of the House of Commons, the second lorry was buffeted by the concussive blast of the first explosion expanding and rolling down the Thames. At first it was the flash that caught the second driver's eye, then the orange ball of fire that erupted into the gray London overcast sky. This being his predetermined signal, the driver closed his eyes and drew a deep breath before muttering a few words, then sent the second lorry loaded with nitrate after the first into oblivion.

———

"Fucking cock," Murphy muttered again as he swung onto the deserted Saint Mary Axe. He was late, and the boss wasn't going to be happy. It wasn't his fault. Christ, there was shit traffic and then the bastard Leadenhall Mob.

He eased the lorry to a halt in the laneway and got out. He looked at his watch.

"Hey, mate, you can't park there. It's blocking the lane."

Murphy turned toward the voice and noticed a police officer wearing a peaked cap and a hi-vis vest walking toward him. He spoke politely. "I'll just be a few minutes, Officer."

"No, mate, move it or I'll book you. You lorry drivers think you can park anywhere. See that?" the policeman said, pointing at the obvious signage right where Murphy had parked.

Shaking his head at the way this was getting out of control, Murphy wondered what else could go wrong. Deciding to get things back on track, the Irishman took a step toward the unsuspecting policeman and drew the

Glock. He shot him twice in the chest and stood over him as he put another bullet in his head, looking around to see who had witnessed his act of violence. Not that it would matter much longer.

Murphy suddenly felt a vibration beneath his feet, and then he heard the distant deep-throated sound of the two explosions. He looked at his watch. "Not much we can do now, boyo," he muttered and started walking away from the lorry.

Five minutes later, London was rocked by a third explosion.

———

BELFAST, IRELAND

Brian Finn, sitting in a comfortable leather chair beside a roaring wood fire with a glass of single malt whiskey in his hand, watched the seventy-inch smart television mounted on the wall in the luxurious living room of his large home. Every now and then, his eyes flicked down to take in the news ticker running its constantly updated cycle along the bottom of the screen. It told him the current count sat at two hundred seventy dead, with many more wounded. Most casualties were from the two bridges. The third lorry bomb explosion had caused considerably less. Finn, however, was not concerned about the body count. The message associated with the third explosion was the one he wanted to be understood.

They were back and they had an ax to grind with anyone who stood in their way. Their message was clear, laid bare by the bombing of the Baltic Exchange twenty-one years after the Provisional IRA had done so in 1992.

"Do you think they will take notice, Da?" Kyran Finn asked his father.

"They fucking better," Finn growled at his son. "But should they not, we have measures in place to ensure their attention. Aren't there?" His eyes narrowed.

"Yes. I got word earlier today. All is ready should the conference go ahead."

"Good."

"The other attacks coincided nicely. With any luck, responsibility for the three will be linked together."

"I don't care if they aren't," Finn said. "I don't care who knows who is responsible, as long as it can't be traced back to me."

"I made sure of that."

Finn leaned forward in his chair. When he spoke, his voice was low and menacing. "How?"

"By cleaning the trail."

The older man's eyes widened, removing the wrinkles from around them. He threw the half-full glass at his son as rage overcame him. "You fucking gobshite, what did you do?"

The glass missed Kyran's head by mere inches, and the liquid splashed his face. He spluttered and exclaimed, "I was just protecting you!"

"Grow a bloody brain, Kyran. I've known Bob Murphy ever since the early days when we did jobs together. He deserves better than a bullet from you for doing what was asked of him. He's loyal to the cause."

"He is a loose end."

"Oh, fuck off," Finn swore, spittle flying from his mouth. "You stop it, Kyran. Stop it right now, or I'll flay you within an inch of your life, and your sister won't be able to save you. Who did you send?"

"Braden."

"Well, call him off."

"I-I can't."

"You'd better, boyo. You'd bloody better."

———

LONDON

Murphy sat on the edge of the hotel bed, watching the twenty-four-hour newsfeed from the BBC. The scenes brought back memories from when he was a boy, in the old days when the IRA was in full swing. When he and Brian Finn ran together. Things were different now, though. Finn was a big man, while he was still the soldier, battered and getting on in years.

But he was giving it one last hurrah before the old feller upstairs came knocking. He switched the channel and found the new feed to be a mirror image of the other. A news camera panned across the Waterloo Bridge. Both middle spans were gone, having fallen into the Thames. Watercraft searched tirelessly up and down the waterway, looking for survivors. The same was happening at Westminster Bridge.

An hour before, the prime minister had made a brief statement, as had the commissioner of the Metropolitan Police. Since then, everything had been speculation.

So engrossed was he in the news feed on his television, Murphy didn't notice the door to the hotel room opening quietly and allowing a slight breeze to flow through. His gaze remained fixed, watching intently for the newscast to cut back to the bomb scene at the Baltic Exchange.

He sensed the danger before he saw it, but by then, it was too late. The shooter raised the suppressed Beretta and was about to fire when Murphy turned. His eyes widened with shock when he saw the face behind the gun, and his expression changed to a snarl. "You fucking gobshite bast—"

Murphy's head snapped back when the bullet punched into it. He fell to the floor with a dull thud and didn't move again. Braden O'Connor unscrewed the suppressor from his handgun and put the two items into separate pockets of his khaki coat. As he did so, the cell in his jeans pocket buzzed. He reached in and took it out. "Yeah?"

He listened in silence for a moment, then said, "It's too late. Job's done."

———

SECURITY SERVICE BUILDING (MI5), LONDON

The secure phone on the desk of Frank Fitzgerald rang twice before he picked it up. It was one of three that sat atop the polished wood surface. This one was a direct line to 10 Downing Street. He picked it up and said, "Sir?"

"How goes it, Frank?" Prime Minister Howard Potter asked in his familiar gravelly voice.

"We're trying to work through the problem, sir. We're liaising with the Met, but it's a lot of work."

"I have an idea, Frank. Hear me out. I was told by Roger over at MI6 about Global Corporation and their newly acquired team. Apparently, they're good at what they do. They got the Ghost and put paid to Ellen Grayson. I was thinking maybe you could use them."

"Are we sure we want to go down that route, sir?" Fitzgerald asked. "Mercenaries on home soil."

"These were the people who saved Her Majesty from a nuclear attack,"[1] Potter said.

This got Fitzgerald's attention. "Reaper, sir. Is that them?"

"That's them, Frank."

"All right, sir. I'll see what I can do."

"Good man. Reach out, use them. Use every asset we can to hunt down those responsible."

"Yes, Prime Minister."

The phone went dead, and Fitzgerald hung up. He pressed the button on the intercom. "Mary, I need you to dig up all you can on a team of specialists named Team Reaper. You've got five minutes."

"Yes, sir."

Five minutes later, a slim woman in her early forties entered with an armful of files. She put them on Fitzgerald's desk and walked out. The Secret Service head picked the top folder and opened it. Staring at him from a black and white picture was a woman in her early forties with long dark hair. Her eyes were brown, and she wore the uniform of a General. He looked at the bottom of the picture; her name was Mary Thurston.

He placed the file to one side and picked up another. This time the picture had *John Kane* written on it. He skimmed through a page of information about the former Recon Marine, then placed it on top of the other. For the next twenty minutes, Fitzgerald pored over each of the files. When he was finished, he sat back in his chair and rubbed a hand over his face, hoping he was making the right decision. Then he reached for his phone.

———

HEREFORD, ENGLAND

Mary Thurston picked up her office phone four hours after the initial call was made to the Global Corporation. She'd been working her way through request forms for the team's armory submitted by Cara. In the corner, a muted television showed running coverage of the bombings in London.

"Thurston," she answered.

"Mary, Hank Jones. I'm sorry it's late, but we have a request from MI5 to attend a briefing in London." Hank Jones was the former United States Chairman of the Joint Chiefs. Now he oversaw Global, having been headhunted by the corporation's owner, George Peacock. To anyone who knew the big man, he bore an uncanny resemblance to General Norman Schwarzkopf Jr., the officer who'd led the coalition forces in the First Gulf War.

"Is it about the bombing, sir?"

"Yes. Put your people on standby, Mary. I'll be there in thirty minutes to get you."

"Yes, sir."

The call disconnected, and Thurston made a call to Ferrero. "Luis, it's time to go to work. I'm going to London. Get the team ready."

---

1. See *Empty Quiver*

CHAPTER 2

"THIS IS MARY THURSTON," Jones said to Fitzgerald. "She's in charge of the team."

The MI5 boss looked her over briefly before taking her hand. "Pleased to meet you. Take a seat."

They sat down.

"Your reputation precedes you," Fitzgerald said. "Especially those of your operators. Just to make this clear, this wasn't my idea. The prime minister called me and wanted to let you loose, so to speak. I think we can handle it, but the old boy wants to use whatever he can get his hands on."

"We'll help anyway we can," Mary said.

Fitzgerald let out a sigh. "Where to start?"

"The beginning is always good," Thurston replied.

"Yes, quite. All right, as you know, earlier today we had three bombs go off in the city. One each on the Westminster and Waterloo Bridges and the other near, or rather outside, the Baltic Exchange."

The MI5 boss had a laptop computer in front of him, and he turned it around. Thurston and Jones watched the feed, and the former asked the obvious question. "Why did that driver get out and kill the police officer before walking away?"

"That is the million-pound question."

"He didn't need to. All he had to do was detonate the bomb. Job done."

"Maybe he had a change of heart," Fitzgerald suggested. From the expression on his face, Thurston could tell he didn't believe it.

She said, "He wasn't part of the terror cell."

The MI5 boss nodded. "So it would seem. We can't get an image of his face."

"It's a mighty big coincidence that this all happened at the same time," Jones pointed out.

"Too big in my book."

Thurston looked stoic. "If it wasn't a coincidence, then it was planned that way. That means someone else knew about the attack before it happened. Has anyone claimed responsibility?"

"No. That's the troubling part. What's your experience with Middle East terror cells?"

"That they usually operate with more than two people," Jones said. "And that being the case, I would hazard a guess and say there are at least three and maybe five more out there somewhere."

"Which means we can expect more attacks."

"Where do you want us to start, Mr. Fitzgerald?" Thurston asked.

"I'm reluctant to let the SAS loose in the city at the moment. They're going through an issue relating to an operation in Libya. How are your intelligence-gathering capabilities?"

Thurston thought of Swift. "My man is good, sir."

"Fine. I'll have my people share what we know with you, and if you're able to find anything at all, then as you Americans say, keep us in the loop."

Thurston stared at him for a moment. "Sir, if we have to go operational in the city, is there going to be a problem?"

"Only if you do more damage than the people you're chasing," Fitzgerald replied. "Just run it past me."

"Will do."

"If you have any issues, I'm always here, but from what I know of Global, you should be right. Like I said, just keep me in the loop."

"Yes, sir."

———

TEAM REAPER HQ, HEREFORD, ENGLAND

"All right, people, gather around," Thurston said as she entered the new operations room. "Slick, did you get the files from MI5?"

"Yes, ma'am. I've been going through them," said the red-headed computer tech.

"Anything stick out?"

"Only like dogs' balls, ma'am."

"All right, we'll get to that in a moment." She turned her gaze on Kane. "The team ready?"

The former Recon Marine nodded. A large Grim Reaper tattoo on his back was the origin of his tag, 'Reaper'. "We're good to go, General."

Beside him stood Cara Billings, one-time Marine lieutenant, former deputy sheriff, now Kane's second in command. "Ma'am, when can we expect our weapons and such to arrive?"

"I've been assured that everything you requested will be here this morning."

"And the medical supplies, ma'am?" Richard 'Brick' Peters asked hopefully. In a former life, the big, bald, bearded man had been a combat medic. Now he did it for the team.

"That too, Brick. Anything else?" Her gaze settled on the two wild men of Team Reaper, Axel 'Axe' Burton and Raymond 'Knocker' Jensen. Both had backgrounds in Special Forces, the latter with the British SAS. "No?"

"Now that you mention it," Axe started, but a hard stare from Thurston stopped him. "Nothing at all, ma'am?"

"What about you, Raymond?"

The tall and solidly built Axe dug Knocker in the ribs with an elbow. "She called you Raymond. Ha-ha."

Knocker was still getting over his kidnapping and torture by the terrorist known as the Ghost. His feet were healing slowly, as was the rest of his body, but he still suffered some pain when he moved. "Good to go, ma'am."

Thurston gave him a skeptical look. "We'll see."

"I'm in better nick than spud-nugget here, ma'am." His thumb indicated his team member standing beside him.

Axe stared at him, a confused look on his face. "What?"

"No time to explain, mate. Just put a sock in your pipe and listen."

"Ma'am," said a woman with long black hair and an athletic build, "we're still waiting on word about a UAV."

Brooke Reynolds, Bravo One, was their UAV pilot. Beside her stood her second seat, Pete Teller.

Thurston looked at Luis Ferrero, her second in command. He shrugged. "I've been assured that we'll be able to access one when required."

"What kind?"

"I was told it would be a Protector?"

"Thanks."

"I know this has been a tough transition," Thurston said. "Not of our choosing. But all we can do is make the best of it. All right, let's start with the briefing."

Moving closer together, they gathered around a large screen. "As you all know, three bombs went off in London yesterday. You've seen the figures. The general and I were called into MI5 last evening, and the head shed asked for our help. This one caught their attention."

Footage of the Baltic Exchange attack appeared on the screen. They watched it in silence before the screen went dark. "Thoughts?" Thurston asked.

"The bastard is Irish," Knocker said, his voice leaving no doubt.

"What makes you say that?" Ferrero asked.

"I just know."

"He could be right," Swift said. "The Exchange was bombed back in 1992 by the Provisional Irish Republican Army."

"Tell them what the date was, Slick," Knocker said.

"Tenth of April."

"And yesterday was?"

"The tenth of April."

"Coincidence? I think not."

"All right," Thurston said. "We'll assume you're right. I want a list of all active IRA people on my desk inside two hours."

"This would indicate that whoever put that truck—sorry, I mean lorry—in place was aware of the other imminent attacks," Kane said, proud of his grasp on the new lingo.

"That's what MI5 thinks."

Cara stepped forward. "Can you put the lorry back up, Slick?"

"Yes, ma'am."

The picture appeared on the screen.

"Now put up the other two."

The screen split into thirds. "There," Cara said, pointing. "Is it just me?"

"No," said Reynolds. "They're the same."

"Alright, let's start there. We find out where the lorries came from, and we also see if we can identify the driver of the third vehicle."

"Ma'am, I might know someone who could assist us with identifying where the lorries came from," Knocker said, putting his hand up as though he were a schoolboy trying to get the teacher's attention.

"Hand down, Knocker. That's fine. You and Reaper go ahead of the rest of us. We'll be relocating to London tomorrow for the duration. Get your kits ready."

"What is it the MI5 is doing, ma'am?" Axe asked, a curious look on his face.

"Looking over our shoulders."

———

LONDON, ENGLAND

It was an old out-of-the-way garage with three mechanics working on automobiles. When the musta-chioed man looked up from beneath the hood of a black Mercedes, he blinked twice and said, "Oh, fuck no."

"Hi there, Robbie, old cock. How's it hanging?" Knocker asked with a broad grin.

"Piss off, Knocker. I don't know nothing, and if I did, I still wouldn't."

"That's no way to speak to an old friend," Knocker said.

"You're no fucking friend, you scouser," Robbie Hunter growled.

Kane stood back and watched them interact, aware of the Glock 19 nestled against his spine. Knocker glanced around the garage. "You've got some nice sets of wheels inside, Robbie. Do the owners know they're here?"

"What are you saying, Knocker?" the mechanic asked indignantly.

"Just admiring the vehicles, Robbie. Like that Mercedes you're working on. Must be worth all of eighty thousand quid. Tell me, why would anyone with a lick of sense let a fucking cow turd like you work on it?"

Kane saw the other two men straighten and take a couple of steps toward the former SAS man. Knocker turned his head and stared hard at them. "Unless you lot want to end up in the closest A&E, I suggest you back the hell away."

They stopped their advance but remained where they stood.

"Now, where was I? That's right. I'm guessing, Robbie, if I have a look in the engine bay, it'll be empty. Am I right?"

"Knocker—"

"No need to say anything. I'm not here to judge. Just looking for a little information, and then I'll leave."

"What information?"

Knocker retrieved a picture from the inside pocket of his coat and passed it to Robbie. The mechanic took it in his greasy hand and studied it. A flicker of recognition in his eyes told Knocker he knew what he was looking at. "Where did they come from?"

"Shit, I don't fucking know, Knocker."

"Come on, Robbie. You must know something. You hear things."

"Sure, I do. But not this."

"Really?"

Robbie glanced at his two mechanics. Knocker caught him and said, "You two, fuck off."

"What?" Robbie blurted, surprised by the order.

"Go on."

The two men looked at their boss. Knocker drew his Glock and pointed it in their direction. "You scousers hard of hearing, huh?"

They held up their hands at shoulder height. One of them, a man with a Welsh accent, said, "Hold fast, mate. We're going. No need to be rash."

Kane kept a keen eye on the pair as they left, his hand resting on the Glock behind his back. Once they were gone, he began to relax. Meanwhile, Knocker had lowered his weapon and was once again focused on the mechanic. "Now, you were saying?"

"Okay, I may have heard something, Knocker."

"Oh, really? Such as?"

"There was a whisper a couple of weeks ago about a guy looking for three lorries. That was what I heard."

Kane stepped closer. "What was the name of the guy?"

"I don't know."

The Team Reaper commander stepped closer and slapped the mechanic across the face. "Try again."

"What the hell, man? You can't do that?" he whined, putting his hands up in front of his face defensively even though the gesture was too late.

"Then talk to us," Knocker said. "By the way, his name is Reaper. You don't want to know why."

Kane stepped closer until his chest was almost touching Robbie's. "All right, man. Just back off."

"Come on, Robbie. Time is wasting."

"Eddie Thomas."

"Yes, keep going."

"Eddie Thomas works out of a warehouse over at Surrey Docks."

"What does he do?" Knocker asked.

The mechanic said nothing.

"Robbie, Robbie, do you want him to get angry?"

Shaking his head nervously, the mechanic answered, "He sells stolen shit."

"Like lorries?" Knocker suggested.

"Yeah, that and other shit."

"He have anyone working for him?" the Brit asked, liking the flow of information he had elicited.

Robbie nodded.

"They armed?"

"Maybe."

"All right. I want an address, and don't get any ideas about warning him. If anything goes wrong, I'll come back here and put a bullet in your head, understand?"

"S-sure, Knocker."

The former SAS man turned to Kane. "You want to rough him up a little? Break his leg or something?"

Robbie's face paled. "What? Wait a minute, I—"

"No," Kane replied, turning away from the mechanic.

"Suit yourself," Knocker said, placing his hands on his hips and fixing the guy with a hard stare. "Remember what I said, Robbie."

"Sure, Knocker. Sure."

The pair walked outside. "You think he was telling the truth?" Kane asked.

"Yeah. He knows what he'll get if he lies to me."

Kane touched his earpiece. "Reaper One to Zero, over."

"I've got you, Reaper One."

"We've got some information we're about to follow up on."

"That's good, Reaper One. Your trackers are working, so we can follow your progress from here. Give me the location, and I'll dispatch the others to help out."

"Roger that." Kane gave him the details, then asked, "Any more news, Luis?"

"Not yet. Zero, out."

Kane and Knocker climbed into a dark blue Range Rover, one of several supplied for their use by the corporation. The former SAS operator drove.

An hour later, they pulled up outside a large warehouse that had once serviced the river trade on the Thames. Before getting out of their vehicle, they checked their weapons. Kane said into his comms, "Reaper Two, are you onsite?"

"Just arriving now."

A dark-colored Range Rover pulled in beside them, and the remaining Team Reaper operators alighted. Kane and Knocker joined them, and they went behind their vehicles.

"Ready to go?" Kane asked Cara.

"And then some," she replied with a grin.

They opened the back of each Range Rovers and started donning their equipment. Once his body armor was on, Kane picked up his main weapon. It was an M6A2 carbine chambered for 5.56 caliber rounds. He placed his Glock in the thigh holster.

This was how they'd chosen to roll on this one. No need for a sniper or a SAW (Squad Automatic Weapon).

"The building we're after is a bit farther along," Kane said. "You've all got pictures of the guy we're after?"

"Yes. Is Slick up and running?" Cara asked.

"Bravo Four, copy?"

"Read you Lima Charlie, Reaper One."

"Do you have eyes on the target building, over?"

"Roger that. I see two guards outside. Both are armed, over."

"Roger that. Let's move out."

———

"What a load of fucking bollocks," Dave Ripley said to Lyle Yates. "How on earth does a scouser like that become the head of South Hampton?"

"He was probably sticking his dick in the old guy's daughter," Lyle replied.

Ripley looked over his shoulder and grinned. "Speaking of sticking your dick in something. Get a look at this cow."

Yates turned to stare in the direction his friend was. Coming toward them dressed in painted-on jeans and a skintight T-shirt was a woman with short, dark hair and a killer body.

"How'd you like to stick your dick in that, Lyle?"

"Hello, boys," she greeted them, her American accent unmistakable. "I'm lost. I'm hoping that maybe you might help me?"

Cara batted her eyelids at them. The ruse was an old favorite, but it was amazing how often it worked. After all, the average male thought about sex nine times a day. That, coupled with the sight of Cara's erect nipples poking through the tightly stretched fabric, and the pair were putty in her hands.

"We'd be happy to help you, luv," Ripley replied, tidying his hair as he leered at her breasts.

Cara stepped forward while reaching behind her back for the map that was tucked into her pocket next to the Glock in her waistband. Her eyes remained focused on the two MP7s the men were armed with.

"Those sure are nice big weapons you boys have there," she said sweetly.

Yates grinned wickedly. "I've got a bigger weapon if you'd like to see it."

"Really?" She stared at them, wide-eyed with incredulity.

"Oh, yes. It's sure to make your eyes pop."

"Come on, Cara, would you stop playing around?" Kane said in her ear.

But it's so much fun. "Show me." Her tone was flirtatious.

Without any hesitation, Yates let his MP7 hang by its shoulder strap and started to undo his pants.

Ripley stared at his friend in disbelief. "What the fuck are you doing?"

"The lady wants to see a big weapon, so I thought I'd oblige."

While they were distracted, Cara reached behind her back and took out her Glock. "Is it bigger than this one?" she asked innocently, aiming the gun at them.

The men froze.

"Oops," she said with a grin. "Somebody screwed up."

Four armed men appeared behind her.

"What the fuck is going on?" Ripley demanded.

"Get on the ground," Knocker growled, relieving him of his weapon.

The men were pushed onto their stomachs before having their hands zip-tied behind their backs. After being assisted to their feet, they were gagged and placed against the wall of the building.

Knocker stood over them. "One squeak out of you two, and I'll see that you get at least twenty years at Her Majesty's pleasure."

With the guards secured, they got ready to breach.

Using two large lorries for cover, they entered silently. Not far beyond them, they detected a couple of men standing by a pallet, one armed, the other not. Against the far wall, a set of stairs climbed to a second-floor office with large windows overlooking the warehouse floor. Kane noticed a flicker of movement from the office window and held a hand up to halt his team. No one spoke, just waited for the all-clear.

Meanwhile, a figure appeared close to one of the windows and stood looking out. While half a minute ticked by, they silently waited for him to walk away.

Kane turned to Knocker. "Take Brick and clear the office up top. We don't have eyes on our target, so be careful. We want him alive."

The team emerged from behind the pair of lorries. Their advance was immediately spotted by the two men on the warehouse floor. The man who was armed tried to get his weapon into action but never had a chance. Kane's suppressed M6 put two bullets into his chest. The man he'd been talking to was fumbling with something under his coat. Cara had him in her sights; had him cold. "Don't do it," she said in a low voice.

He heard the voice and chose to ignore it; the man kept working at what he was doing. His hand appeared, filled with a gun. Cara muttered a curse as he started to bring it up, then she put him down. "Dickhead. You could have lived."

"Secure the floor," Kane ordered.

Over at the far wall, Knocker and Brick started up the stairs. They moved with practiced ease, if not cat-like grace. At the top, they paused briefly outside the door before entering. Knocker turned the handle while Brick breached the flimsy laminate barrier.

Sweeping the room, Brick took in the target sitting

behind the desk and another man standing beside a cupboard, holding an open folder.

"Hold it there!" Brick shouted, adding to the surprise.

Knocker emerged from behind him and started toward the immobile men. He pointed at the man with the folder. "You, get on the floor."

The man stared in shock at the business end of the M6 in the operator's hands. Knocker growled, "Come on, mate, we've not got all day. Now get your arse down on the sodding floor."

The man dropped the folder to the cracked linoleum tiles and dove down beside it. Still in his chair, Eddie Thomas finally found his voice. "What the fuck is this? What do you think you're doing?"

"Shut up," Brick ordered. "Now, join your friend there on the floor."

As he did so, Brick said into his comms, "Reaper One, we've got the target in custody."

"Roger that. Bring him down; the main building is clear."

"We'll be down directly," he responded, then turned to the prisoners. "Right, you lot, on your feet." To his partner, he said, "Move them on down, Knocker. The boss wants a word."

———

After they descended to the cavernous warehouse space downstairs, Brick manhandled Thomas into a chair and refastened his hands behind the metal frame.

Kane said, "Axe, stand guard out front. Brick, take the back." Both operators disappeared to their designated positions. Kane stood in front of Thomas and fixed him with a withering stare. He kept it up for at least a minute before Thomas blurted, "Who are you bloody wankers?"

"You don't get to ask the questions," Kane said.

"You don't know who you're dealing with, mother—"

Knocker slapped him on the back of his head. "You got that wrong, cock. You screwed up royally, and we're about the only ones who can help you. Whether we choose to is another matter."

"Help me? What do you mean?"

"Well, if British intelligence gets you, mate, you won't see daylight for at least fifty years. Maybe longer."

"What? What for?" Thomas gasped.

"Your part in the bombing, of course," Kane replied.

A look of horror crossed his face. "Wait a minute, I never had nothing to do with that."

"So you admit it, then? If you never had nothing to do with it, that is an admission of guilt in my book. A double negative makes a positive. You need to learn to speak English a bit better," Cara said.

The man looked at her dumbly, not understanding the meaning of her words.

"You supplied the lorries," Cara said, moving on. "In the eyes of the Security Service, that makes you part of it. They'll lock you in a small room and waterboard you until you speak."

"They can't do that!"

"You're a terrorist, Eddie," Cara hissed, getting up in his face. "You've had it."

"No, I'm not." The denial came out as a wheedle.

Cara gave him a sad look. "Yes, honey. You're screwed."

Thomas became even more confused as he contemplated the trouble he was in.

Kane said, "Tell us about the lorries."

Thomas' shoulders slumped. "I-I was asked to get them. But you must understand, I didn't know what they were for."

"Now you do, you bloody tosser," Knocker growled. "Who wanted them?"

Thomas hesitated. "I don't know his name."

"Fuck off, Thomas. If you'd answered straight away, I might have believed you. But you hesitated. That tells me you're lying. Try again."

"Bobby Murphy."

"Who's Bobby Murphy?" Knocker asked.

"He's old-school Irish."

Knocker moved closer. "IRA?"

"Years ago. Provisional, I think."

"An old hand from PIRA comes to you to get him three lorries, and it fails to trigger anything with you?" The former SAS man growled, "Are you some kind of dickhead or what?"

"It's the truth!" Thomas explained. "And it was four, not three."

Knocker glanced at Kane. "Did he just say four?"

"I think so."

"It was definitely four," Cara confirmed.

Kane swore vehemently. "Who picked them up?"

"I don't know. We just dropped them off and left them."

"Where?"

"Woolwich."

"I need an address," Kane demanded menacingly.

Thomas rattled it off. Kane said into his comms, "Bravo Four, copy?"

"I'm here, Reaper One."

"I have an address for you in Woolwich. You're looking for another lorry."

"Say again, Reaper?"

"You heard me right. There were four lorries, not three. I'm thinking they had a place nearby."

"Roger that," Swift said. "I'll see what I can come up with."

"Thanks, Slick. Let the boss know we'll be back shortly with our prisoner. And let MI5 know they might want to send a cleanup team here."

"On it. Out."

"Reaper One, out."

CHAPTER 3

LONDON, ENGLAND

FRANK FITZGERALD, escorted by Traynor, entered the ops room. The former DEA undercover agent showed him over to where Thurston was talking to Kane. After turning to meet them, Thurston introduced him to Kane. "Mr. Fitzgerald, this is John Kane, my team commander."

They shook hands. "Frank Fitzgerald. Pleased to meet you."

"You too, sir."

"I hear you have a man in custody who gave you a lead."

"We're still questioning him, but he's being cooperative."

"What has he said so far?" Fitzgerald asked. "Has he given you any names?"

"We're working on it. We know the name of the guy who ordered the four lorries."

The MI5 commander raised his eyebrows. "Four?"

"Yes."

"Good Lord. We feared that might be the case."

"We have a drop-off location for them, and our tech is going through feed, trying to locate those responsible."

"What was the name of the person who ordered the lorries?"

"An Irishman called Bob Murphy. He's an old PIRA."

"Shit. I'll have my people look into him."

Swift appeared. "I have a location for Bob Murphy."

"Where?" Thurston asked.

"A hotel in Blackheath."

Thurston looked at Kane. "Get over there and bring him in. Alive. Take Cara and Knocker with you."

"Yes, ma'am."

"Be careful," Fitzgerald cautioned him. "If the PIRA is becoming active again, you could be walking into something bigger than you think."

Kane nodded. "I'll keep that in mind."

After her team commander had gone, Thurston asked, "Is there a reason the PIRA might be raising their heads at this particular time?"

Fitzgerald stared at her in silence.

"Come on, Frank. If we're going to succeed in this, I need to hear everything so I can brief my people."

Fitzgerald sighed. "All right, but this is top secret."

"I trust my people."

"Sometime over the next week, there is to be a meeting of Irish and British dignitaries at a secret location in London. They will be discussing the possible unification of the North with the rest of Ireland."

Thurston was confused. "Isn't that a good thing? That's what they've fought for over so many years."

"There is a condition," Fitzgerald said. "For the first five years, the whole of united Ireland will be under the rule of the British government. Ireland is in dire economic trouble and has reached out for help. The deal on the table is that they can have a united Ireland, but the government wants to oversee everything for the next five years and help them get back on their financial feet."

"Obviously, word has gotten out, and the bombing of the Exchange is a warning, I'd say. If there is another lorry out there somewhere, it's possible that they intend to use it," Thurston mused.

"But we don't know if they have it. For all we know, the terrorists who struck the bridges could have it."

"Who was the PIRA affiliated with back in the day?"

"Everyone they were affiliated with has been disbanded in the intervening years. However, now that you mention it, if I had to put someone at the top of the list, I would say Libya."

"Is there a reason for that conclusion?" Thurston asked.

"Three months ago, British Intelligence received word about an HVT in Tobruk. It was confirmed, and an SAS team was inserted and made their way to the target house. Something went wrong, and everything fell apart. Civilians were killed, but they missed the HVT. Hence the investigation underway, and why you were brought in instead of them."

"So, what you're saying is, this could be a revenge strike?" Thursday eyed him incredulously.

"Yes."

Thurston nodded. "All right, say it is. How did they get into the country?"

"Good question." The man shrugged and moved his hands palms up in the universal symbol for "who knows?"

Ferrero appeared just as Fitzgerald's cell went off. "There's been another explosion in London."

"Where?"

"Epsom. From what I can gather, Specialist Firearms Command and Counter-Terrorist Specialist Firearms officers stormed a warehouse. They got inside, and whatever was in there went off. There were a lot of casualties."

Fitzgerald finished his phone call, and within moments, Thurston saw the dark side of the outwardly quiet man. He glowered at her. "I have to go. Keep me updated on what you find."

She watched him leave, then turned to Ferrero. "Keep the comms open on Kane and Cara and have Slick find me all he can about the operation conducted by the SAS in Libya a few months back."

"Yes, ma'am. Anything specific he should be looking for?"

"Yes. I want the name of the HVT."

"On it."

———

When it arrived on the fifth floor, the elevator's bell dinged, and the doors opened to disgorge its load. Three people alighted and moved silently down the hallway, stopping once they reached the room they sought. There was one either side of the door, and the third readied to breach. All had their Glock 19s drawn.

Knocker nodded and stepped forward. After a blow from his right boot, the door flew open. Cara was the first through, and a curtain of foul-smelling air hit her in the face. She immediately knew what it was but needed to clear the apartment before doing anything else.

Noticing the corpse on the floor, Cara called, "I've got a body."

Skirting around the death scene, Cara entered the bedroom. She found it empty and returned to the main room. "Bedroom is clear."

Kane said, "So is the bathroom."

Knocker was peering at the body of Murphy on the floor. He wrinkled his nose. "I'd say he didn't live long after the bombing. Someone is covering their tracks."

"You ever know the IRA to shoot one of their own to cover their ass?" Kane asked.

"Nope. I've known them to turn on their own if they feel betrayed."

"I'll call it in. Have a look around."

They spent the next thirty minutes turning the room over but found nothing. Thurston informed Kane that the Met Police would be onsite soon, and once they arrived, the team members would give a statement and return to base.

"Roger that."

Knocker shook his head. "I don't get it. Why kill him?"

Cara shrugged. "All I can come up with is to keep him silent."

"Yeah. It doesn't make sense."

———

"Luis, do you have a moment?"

"Sure, Slick. What is it?" Ferrero asked, turning to face the computer tech.

"I've been looking into the past of the dead Irish guy. I cross-referenced him with known associates and came up with several possibilities, but there's one that stands out."

"Who is that?"

"A guy named Brian Finn."

Ferrero nodded. "What's his history?"

"He owns any number of businesses in London as well as in Belfast. Appears to be worth quite a bit of money. Was imprisoned early in his life in Belfast for shooting a British soldier. Was let out as part of a peace deal a year later. Somewhere along the way, he met up with Bob Murphy. MI5 has records on them as being suspected in a couple more deaths of soldiers, as well as a couple of bombings, one in Belfast, the other in London. They couldn't find anything concrete. They did catch one suspect, but he wouldn't talk. Also suspected of ripping off an arms shipment turned in after one of the peace agreements. Again, the investigation went nowhere. MI5 put a guy in undercover, and he wound up with his throat cut and hanging from a lamp post."

"Do we know where he is?"

"Belfast was the last report I saw."

"Fine. Is there anything else?"

"The general asked me to find out who the Libyan target the SAS went after was, and I think I know."

"Who?"

Swift said, "Hasan Kubar. He's the leader of a terror organization called the Libyan Freedom Fighters. They were responsible for different terror attacks in Europe, and they provided a funnel for arms to terror networks in Nigeria."

"Boko Haram?"

"Among others."

"So this could well be a revenge strike."

"Yes," Swift replied.

"They still had to get into the country somehow," Ferrero pointed out. "We just need to find out how. I'll take this to Mary and see what she wants to do. Good work, Slick."

"Thank you, sir."

Ferrero found her tucked away in a room with Traynor and Arenas, going through reports provided to them by MI5. "This is where you all hang out."

Thurston looked up from the folder she held. "It's mind-numbingly invigorating."

"I might have something to get those synapses firing again," he said with a smile.

She tossed the folder on the table, giving him a tired smile in return. "Anything?"

"Slick found a possible lead to an Irishman named Brian Finn. Former IRA, has done time, released in a peace deal, suspected of a few other things. Lives in Belfast."

"That's interesting."

"Not as interesting as what I've got next. Hasan

Kubar, Libyan terrorist who was the target of the SAS when their operation went south."

Thurston thought for a moment. "All right, here's what we're going to do. We're going to send someone to Belfast to find out all we can about Finn. In addition, we're going to send Reaper to Libya and find Kubar. If we can take him alive, we might just get the information we need about how his men got into the country and confirm that Finn was the one working with him."

"You'll need to run it past Fitzgerald, seeing as we're working with them."

"I'll go see him shortly. In the meantime, when Reaper gets back, have them prepare for deployment."

"I'll see to it."

———

Fitzgerald was busy but made time for Thurston. They sat in his office, and she laid out her plan. "I'm going to send a couple of my men to Ireland to dig around about Finn."

"Save yourself the trouble. My people can tell you what you need to know."

"Maybe, but he's been out of circulation for a while, and I want to know what he's like now," Thurston explained.

He nodded. "All right."

"I'm also sending my combat team to Libya after Hasan Kubar." She waited for his reaction.

"No." The answer was blunt, and from its tone, he would brook no argument.

"If we can get him alive, it might give us what we need to find those responsible on this end."

"We can do that anyway," Fitzgerald said.

"Not necessarily. How many surviving terrorists did you get?" Thurston asked. "Murphy is dead too. There's no one directly linking Finn and the terrorists, and no one linking Finn and the attack on the Exchange because the link is dead. If we get Kubar, it'll kill two birds with one stone."

Fitzgerald relented. "All right. Do it."

CHAPTER 4

OFF THE COAST OF TOBRUK

DEEP in the bowels of the battered old freighter, Kane and the others went over the plan one final time. On the table was a satellite picture with several positions marked on it.

"All right," Kane said. "The Royal Marines will drop us here in this small cove. Once we're ashore, we cross this open ground until we reach the edge of the city. We need to be done before daylight."

"That's the most worrying part of the plan," Cara said. "If we get pinned down for any length of time in the city, we're going to be crossing that in daylight, leaving us exposed as shit."

"Kubar certainly picked where he stays. Not far from the police station," Axe noted. "Have we confirmed whose side they're on?"

"No. We do not engage in a firefight with local law enforcement," Kane's voice was firm.

"Roger that."

"Are we sure he's there?" Knocker asked.

"MI6 has him there as of thirty minutes ago. If there is any change, they'll reach out to Bravo, who will then contact us. Remember, this is as black as they come. If we get caught, we're on our own. We're totally deniable."

He smiled and looked at Kane. "It's starting to feel like home already."

"We need Kubar alive. If we can't do that, then it's the long way around to get answers. That leads to the possibility of more people dying."

A Royal Marine lieutenant appeared at the hatch. "We're ready to go, chaps...and lass."

"We'll be on deck in a couple of mikes," Kane said.

"We'll be waiting."

They grabbed their gear. Kane, Brick, and Knocker were armed with suppressed M6A2 carbines. Axe, as usual, carried the SAW. Cara had herself a new sniper system. Whereas before she'd worked with the M110A1, she was now armed with a L129A1 Designated Marksman Rifle. Chambered for 7.62, it was heavy but comfortable to use.

Once they had their gear, they went topside, where they found the Royal Marines waiting for them with a RHIB on the seaward side of the ship. It was this they would use to insert the team onto the shore at Tobruk.

They climbed into the RHIB, and it was lowered over the side. The boat had a crew of three. Just before they hit the water, the motor was started. On touchdown, the boat was disconnected, the driver thrust the throttles forward, and it sped away from the freighter.

There was a small swell on the sea, and the RHIB occasionally skipped as it motored toward shore. Kane could feel the occasional hit of saltwater spray as it went along. The team had night-vision goggles but didn't have them pulled down. On the other hand, the Royal Marines did.

Ten minutes later, Kane's comms came to life with a British voice. "One minute."

Each member of the team lowered their NVGs, flicked their weapons off safe, and prepared to land.

———

TOBRUK, LIBYA

Team Reaper waited for the sound of the retreating RHIB to fade before moving. Cara had made her way to the top of the sandstone embankment and lay prone, using her scope to sweep the terrain ahead. She pressed the talk button on her comms. "Reaper One, all clear."

The others made their way to her position and lay beside her. In the distance, the lights of the city were visible. The ground between the beach and the city was clear. "All right," Kane said in a soft voice, "Knocker, on point. Brick, rear security. Move out."

Their progress was smooth and uninterrupted. They reached the outskirts of the city and regrouped. From there, it was a matter of traversing narrow streets and alleys covered with garbage and the odd stray dog.

"Hold." The voice was urgent and soft.

"What is it?" Kane asked Knocker.

"I've got two civilians close by, shooting the shit."

"We'll have to go around," Kane said. "On me."

They backtracked for a hundred meters or so before

changing direction, giving the two civilians a wide berth.

It took a further thirty minutes to reach the target building.

In an alley just shy of it, they stopped. Kane said into his comms, "Bravo Four? Reaper One. Do you have eyes on the target, over?"

"Roger that, Reaper One. ISR has two guards out front and possibly three tangos inside. The surrounding buildings are also occupied. Watch your back."

"Understood. Reaper One, out."

Kane turned to Cara. "Take up position across the street. If anything comes along, let us know."

"Roger that."

Knocker was the first out of the alley, with his M6 at his shoulder in the firing position. The suppressed weapon spat rounds, and the first guard jerked and fell. Kane followed him, dropping the second guard on the stoop.

Cara found a good position to hunker down and waited for the rest of the team to do their thing as they prepared to breach.

Knocker set the explosive charge and stepped to the side until he was clear. Kane tapped him on the shoulder, and he blew the door.

The former SAS man entered the building, and he came under fire almost immediately. At the end of the hallway stood a shooter, blazing away with an AK47. Something had warned them. Maybe there were motion sensors or a camera they hadn't picked up. Whatever it was, things had quickly turned to shit.

Knocker backpedaled as rounds whizzed past him

dangerously close. He took cover beside the door. "Fuck me!" he exclaimed. "This is going to be a dog's dinner."

He leaned around the opening and let loose a burst of his own. The bullets missed, the shooter wisely having taken cover.

"Reaper, flash-bang!"

Kane took one from his webbing and pulled the pin, then tossed it into the hall and waited. After it had detonated, Knocker entered. The shooter was stunned, and the former SAS man put him down with two shots.

"Reaper One, we've got squirters out the back," Swift said into his ear.

"Motherfucker," Kane growled. "Knocker, squirters out the back."

"On it."

The Brit traversed the hall, stepping over the prone body of the terrorist, until he found the kitchen. It was empty. He pressed forward and out through an open rear door that led into an alley. In his headset, he heard Kane say, "Reaper Two, regroup on us. We're headed out the back in pursuit of the squirters."

"Copy, Reaper."

As soon as Knocker emerged from the rear of the building, another AK opened up. This time, however, the shooter was screaming as well. From what Knocker knew of the language, they were calling for help.

The Brit rolled behind a pile of crates. Round after round shattered the wood, sending sharp splinters scything through the air.

"Shit a fucking brick, could this get any better?" he growled. He looked at the doorway he'd just passed through. Kane emerged and opened fire with his M6.

The shooter was already running, his brief act of bravery done with. Or maybe it was because of what was about to happen.

An RPG round streaked out of the darkness and punched into the side of the building. Kane saw it coming more by good luck than anything else. He shouted a warning and threw himself to the ground.

The explosion was deafening. His ears rang as debris rained down. Kane felt something hit his ballistic helmet and turned to spy a decent-sized chunk of masonry. He coughed dust from his lungs. "All callsigns report. Fuck."

"Two, okay."

"Three, okay."

"Four, okay."

"Five, okay."

"Knocker, where did it come from?"

"The alley at our two o'clock."

"Bravo Four, do you have him?"

"Reaper, I have tangos popping all over the screen," Swift said.

"Shit. Can you see where Kubar went?"

"Negative. Like I said, there are tangos everywhere. They're converging on your position."

"Look for the bastard that is running away from it."

"I've got him, Reaper. Headed southeast."

"Roger that. Reaper One is Charlie Mike."

"Reaper One, this is Bravo, over."

"Read you, Bravo," he told Thurston.

"You need to withdraw, Reaper. Things are getting out of hand."

"Negative, ma'am. We need to scoop this guy up. Request permission to continue?"

After a brief silence and against her better judgment, Thurston came back. "Affirmative, Reaper One. Good luck."

"Knocker, take us southeast. Bravo Four, I need you to keep the reports coming as long as you can."

They cut through alley after narrow alley in pursuit of their quarry. Swift kept the updates coming, but with each one, the situation became a little worse. "Reaper One, the police have deployed, and they seem to be headed your way. I've also got at least twenty tangos converging on your track from the southwest."

"Where is Kubar?"

"About a block ahead of—"

"What is it?" Kane asked when the tech went quiet.

"He's getting into a vehicle, Reaper. You're going to lose him."

"Keep—"

Gunfire rattled from a street as they crossed it, and bullets cracked low overhead. "Take cover!" Kane snapped.

The sound of the suppressed SAW came to him as he opened fire. "Reaper One, troops in contact, over."

"Roger, Reaper One."

"Reaper One, if you can get off the street, do it," Swift said calmly. "I've got a vehicle coming toward your position. Could well be a technical."

"It's a bit hard when we're frigging pinned down, Bravo Four."

"Just the messenger, Reaper One."

The vehicle burst into view. It was a dark 4X4, and mounted on the back was a DShK. "Cor, screw that for a laugh," Knocker growled and opened fire with his M6. Bullets started to ricochet from the vehicle, which came to a sliding stop. Within moments, the DShK opened fire.

Cara brought her DMR up and ground her teeth together, expecting to be cut in half by one of the heavy machine gun rounds. She dropped her sights onto the shooter, and without hesitation, squeezed the trigger.

The man's head snapped back as one of the 7.62 rounds blew his brains out the back of his skull in a fine mist.

The DShK fell silent, but the second man in the back, most likely a loader, scrambled into position. "Not so fast, asshole," Cara breathed, taking up the slack on the trigger of her weapon again.

"Move, Reaper. Get off the street," she called over the comms.

The team came up as one and started to finish their crossing. Swift's voice came over the comms. "Reaper One, the target is now mobile. Headed south out of the city."

"Blast," Kane snapped and turned his head, looking at the technical. "The technical. Go."

The team changed direction toward the vehicle. The driver was dead behind the wheel, the motor still running. Axe dragged the body out and climbed in. Cara jumped into the passenger side while the other got rid of the bodies in the back and hopped in. Cara looked at the former Recon Marine. "No fucking way."

"Hang on, ma'am. We got rabbits to hunt." He floored the accelerator, and the vehicle shot forward. He glanced at Cara. "Where are we going, ma'am?"

"To die, Axe. We're going to fucking die."

The sun came up across the desert early the next morning, offering the promise of another hot day. The team had lost their satellite feed hours before, so now they were relying on instinct. The dirt road before them was full of holes and corrugations. In the passenger seat, Axe sat with his arms folded, pouting like a baby who'd had his toy taken away as punishment. "I can't see why I couldn't keep driving."

Cara looked at him after she'd dodged yet another hole. "You know why."

"It wasn't my fault. The dog ran in front of me."

"There was no dog, Axe."

"Would you believe a donkey?"

"You fucked up. Just face it."

"It wasn't that bad."

"Tell that to the woman's laundry you wiped out," Cara replied.

"She was very understanding, I thought."

"If by understanding you mean coming at you with a large knife, then yeah, she had more than an abundance of understanding. Just face it, Axe; you drive like shit."

"Reaper Two, are you still driving, over?"

"Roger, Bravo Four."

"Thank God."

"I heard that," Axe growled.

"I have satellite back up. About three kilometers ahead of you is a road that turns to your right. It goes on for a couple more kilometers, leading to what appears to be a camp. It looks like your target stopped there."

"What kind of camp, Bravo Four?" Cara asked above the roar of the motor.

"It could be anything, but MI6 has been getting reports of a training camp in that area for the Libyan Independent Brigade."

"Are you telling me that it could be a terrorist camp, Slick?"

"It could well be."

"Reaper, did you get that?"

"I got it, Cara." He paused. "Slick, find us a place to lay up so we can dismount and approach on foot."

"Wait one, Reaper."

The technical hit another hole, and it felt as though the front end had been smashed out of it. Cara guided it to the edge of the road and stopped. Axe gave her a 'Look'. "And you think *I* drive like shit."

"Just shut up, Axe."

Cara knelt at the front of the vehicle. From the back, Knocker called, "You been taking driving lessons from our resident lunatic, love?"

"Hey!" Axe yelled.

Cara got to her feet and glared at the smiling Brit. "Call me love one more time and they'll change your name to Nutless. Everyone out; the front axle is screwed."

Brick slapped Knocker on the back. "After you, Nutless."

"She loves me. I know."

"Keep believing that, Knocker," Cara told him.

"Oh, you're a hard woman," the Brit said, jumping down. He winced when the tender spots in his still-healing feet touched the road.[1]

Cara stared at him. "You all right?"

"Just knackered, ma'am."

"Brick, have a look at his feet."

"I told you I'm fine," he said, waving the former SEAL away.

"Just do it. That's an order."

Knocker looked at Kane for help. Kane shrugged. "You heard her."

"All right. I know when I'm beat."

"Bravo Four, we're not going to need that lay-up area now. We'll be proceeding on foot, over."

"Roger that, Reaper."

"Cara? You want point?"

She nodded. "On it."

She led them across the desert on a direct azimuth toward their target. For the next hour, they made steady progress to a low ridge. Once they made its crest, they sank down to study the camp beyond it. Swift had been right. It *was* a training camp, and there were terrorists everywhere.

———

BELFAST, NORTHERN IRELAND

The pub was called the Republican, and for that reason alone, it stood out.

Troy and Traynor looked at each other as the light drizzle fell around them. Troy said, "As good a place as any, I guess."

"According to MI5, he drops in here occasionally," Traynor replied. "But isn't this a big 'Fuck You' to their friends across the sea?"

When Troy opened the door, a warm rush of air hit

him in the face. The smell of woodsmoke from the open fire came with it. They stepped in and took off their jackets. Of the dozen or so customers enjoying the hospitality, only a couple looked their way. Traynor spotted the open fire, orange flames licking at a large log that had recently been added. On the wall beside the fireplace hung a huge chalkboard, the menu printed neatly in a variety of colored chalk. Traynor asked, "You hungry? It's noon."

"Sure, why not?"

"What's fish and chips?" Traynor asked.

Troy smiled. He'd heard the term before. "Fries."

They walked up to the bar, and a large man came over to serve them. Troy asked, "Could we get something to eat, please?"

The man studied them with a cautious eye. "Maybe. Find a table if you can, and Mary will be out shortly. Drinks?"

Traynor nodded. "Couple of beers?"

The man poured two pints and took their money. Troy and Traynor found a table where they could see the door and any trouble that might come their way. Traynor looked around the room. "They don't like us."

"How can you tell?" Troy asked. "Maybe it's just you."

Troy saw that there were more sour-faced people studying them. "We're American," Troy said. "We hate the British too."

"What the fuck are you doing?" Traynor growled softly.

"Just saying hi."

The blonde-haired, grim-faced waitress came over

to their table. Troy smiled at her and said, "You have a pretty face. You should smile more."

"American?" she asked.

"Yes."

"Figures. What do you want to eat?"

"Fish and chips," Troy said.

"Make that two," Traynor added.

"It'll be fifteen minutes. You want another drink while you wait?" Mary asked, nodding at their half-full glasses.

"We're all right, thanks," Troy said.

She left them and went to the kitchen. Troy nodded at a picture on the wall of the pub. "You seen that guy before?"

"Nope. Who is he?" Pete asked as he downed several mouthfuls of beer, licking his lips when he finished.

"Sean Duffy. One time IRA commander back in the day."

"How do you know that?"

Troy shrugged. "Not sure. Just do. To the Irish, he was a hero. Blew the shit out of a British Military barracks back in the eighties." Troy took a deep draught of beer and set the empty back on the table.

"Nice."

"Well, well," Troy said with cynical amusement. "Look at the picture on the other wall."

Traynor looked and nodded. "It seems Duffy isn't the only hero."

"Finn is too."

"You gents like another beer?" the barman asked as he picked up their empty glasses.

"Sure," Troy said. "We'll have another two."

"Noticed you were looking at the pictures."

"Two of the local heroes?" Troy asked.

"What makes you say that?"

"Just a guess. Duffy for sure. Finn do something as well?"

The man's eyes narrowed. "What are you saying, boyo?"

"No need to get bent out of shape," Traynor said. "We were curious. Everyone knows what Duffy did. What about Finn? I've never heard of him."

"Then how do you know him?" the man sneered.

"That's my fault," Troy replied. "I didn't think he deserved to be hung in the same room as IRA royalty."

"You'd better watch your mouth, mister. Voicing opinions too loud can get a body hurt."

"Hey, I never meant to offend. I was only saying."

"Yeah, well..."

"Does he come in much?" Traynor asked.

"What?"

"Finn. Does he come in? I was only wondering because you have such a high opinion of him."

"What if he does?" the barman asked.

"Just curious. What's he like?"

"None of your damned business."

"Does he still preach the cause? Or is he getting too old?"

"You're never too old for the cause, boyo. And they're about to find out in a big way."

"What do you mean?" Troy asked.

The barman realized he'd said too much. He waved the question away. "Nothing. Just a talkative man letting his mouth run away with him. I'll get you those drinks."

"He knows something," Troy said.

"Look around you," Traynor replied. "You notice anything?"

"What, apart from most of the customers being over fifty and hating us?"

"Yes."

Troy covertly studied the room, then the dime dropped. "You thinking that all these old-timers are attached to the IRA or some of its splinter groups?"

"Maybe not now, but at one time."

The door opened, and two men wearing thick parkas entered. One of them, the older of the two, called as he hung his parka, "Two beers, Colin."

"Sure thing, Mister Finn." The barman glanced at Troy and Traynor.

Troy said, "This is interesting."

The two men sat down at a vacant table. The barman delivered their drinks to them and left. "Do you think he's forgotten our drinks, Troy?" Traynor asked.

"So it would seem."

Mary appeared with their meals. Troy asked, "Is that Brian Finn over there?"

"Maybe."

"Who's the young guy with him?"

"His son, Kyran."

"Does he take after his old man?"

"Enjoy your meals."

They started eating and had to agree the food was good. As they ate, they kept an eye on the far table where the Finns sat. Traynor said, "We're not going to get anything out of anyone here. Not more than what we already have, anyway."

Troy nodded. "We can have Slick look into Kyran; he might come up with something. You done with your meal?"

Traynor saw a look in his eye. "What are you up to?"

Troy came to his feet. "God bless the Queen!"

You could have heard a pin drop as an unearthly silence enveloped the pub. Every head in the room turned to stare at Troy. The barman turned pale, then red. "Out!" he exclaimed, pointing at the door.

"Why?" asked Troy. "Can't a man express his opinion anymore?"

Kyran Finn got out of his seat. "Not in this pub, they can't."

"Then I humbly apologize to you and your father, Mr. Finn."

"Just leave."

Traynor got to his feet. "Maybe it's best."

Troy glanced at him and nodded. "Yeah, maybe you're right."

As they made their way past the Finns' table, Troy asked in a low voice, "Blown anything up lately?"

The stoic expression on the Irishman's face flickered momentarily before the shutters came back down. His son, however, flared like a struck match. "What the fuck did you say?"

Troy looked innocently at Kyran and pointed at himself. "Me?"

"Yes, you. I don't appear to be looking at anyone else, do I?"

Troy glanced at Traynor. "He wasn't talking to you, was he?"

"No. You."

"All right then." Troy sighed. "I was just wanting to know if your dad has blown anything up lately?"

"Shut your gob," Kyran snarled. "Get out of here before you get thrown out."

"I'll take that as a no."

Kyran stepped forward, striking a threatening pose. Troy braced himself. If the younger Finn thought he'd scare easily, he was wrong.

"Kyran," Finn snapped. "Let it be. Sit down."

"But, Da!"

"Just do it."

The younger Finn took his seat. His old man stared at the two Americans. "I'll give you some advice, boyo. Don't get mixed up in another country's politics. Things have a way of turning nasty."

Troy nodded. "I'll keep that in mind."

"Now, after you apologize, be on your way."

Troy gave him a mirthless grin. "Good day to you, Mr. Finn."

Traynor and Troy headed toward the door. Finn called after them, "I didn't hear your apology."

"No, you didn't."

The door closed behind them, and Kyran asked, "What the fuck, Da?"

"Hold your tongue, boy."

"Are you just going to let them get away with that?"

"Shut up, Kyran," Finn hissed. "What you should be concerned with is what they know, not what they said."

"How could they know anything? They're just a couple of Americans."

"If you say so, son. If you say so."

Outside, Traynor glared at Troy. "What was that?"

"Like you said, we weren't going to get anything. However, now that we've poked the bear, we'll see how he reacts."

"Let's hope he doesn't react too hard."

---

1. See *Hunting Ghosts*

CHAPTER 5

BELFAST, NORTHERN IRELAND

"ARE you sure this is the right place?" Kyran asked Paddy O'Malley.

"Aye. We managed to find them," the black-haired thug confirmed. "We tracked them here, right, boyo?"

"That's right," a voice said from the rear of the Land Rover.

There were two carloads of shooters. Eight men in all, including Kyran Finn. "All right, let's go get these bastards."

O'Malley hesitated.

"What's wrong, Paddy?" Kyran asked.

"Are you sure your da will be all right with this, Kyran?"

"Of course, he will be."

"I don't know. Maybe we should just let it go and ask him."

"In case you haven't noticed, Paddy, he's not

fucking here at the moment. Which puts me in charge. If you don't want to do it, just say so and get the fuck out."

A gloomy silence pervaded the Land Rover, everyone there knowing what it meant if Paddy got out. It wouldn't be the first time Kyran's anger had gotten the better of him and he shot one of them—in the back.

"No, it's good. As long as your da is good too."

"Right, then. Get out of the fucking car."

With a collective sigh of relief, they exited the vehicles and walked across the street toward the motel. Each man carried a Steyr AUG A3 Bullpup carbine.

They stopped in the parking lot. "Which room?" Kyran asked.

"Room four," O'Malley replied.

"Good. Let's do it."

———

"Looks like we got a reaction," Traynor said as they peered through a crack in the curtains.

"You think they brought enough firepower?" Troy asked.

Traynor put a round into the breech of his M6 carbine. "I guess we're about to find out."

Kyran and his men opened fire. All hell broke loose as bullets punched through the exterior wall and shattered the window. Troy and Traynor had taken cover behind the bed, and all kinds of debris began to rain down upon them. A mirror on the interior wall shattered, while a microwave on a small bench seemed to explode after a bullet smashed into it. The television did virtually the same thing, while above the two men's heads, holes seemed to grow with the ongoing influx of hot lead.

"These bastards are serious," Troy growled.

Traynor went to rise, wanting to return fire out through the vacant space where the window used to be. Troy grabbed his arm to stop him. "Wait until it stops."

He dropped back down just as a round almost parted what was left of his hair. Troy said, "They'll stop in a minute, thinking they've got us. Then we'll hit them."

Troy was right. Within the next thirty seconds, the firing stopped. Troy nodded at Traynor. "It's time."

They came out from behind the bed and moved to the window opening. Troy peered around the edge of the shattered frame and saw the thugs standing there, weapons lowered. In the meager illumination thrown by the parking lot's lights, he recognized Kyran, who was waving two men forward to check on the results of their ambush.

Troy lined up on the lead man and fired the M6. The man dropped in an untidy heap. Troy shifted his aim before the dead man's inertia had stopped him moving. He squeezed the trigger again, with the same result.

The stunned onlookers moved to bring up their weapons once more to open fire, but by then, Traynor was involved as well. Both men let loose a solid fusillade of fire, killing two more and scattering the rest. Troy and Traynor stopped firing as the four remaining men ran across the street to the waiting vehicles. They leaped in and started them. Within a few heartbeats, they were gone.

Troy turned to Traynor. "You'd best call the boss.

I'm thinking we're going to get a lot of grief from the locals."

LONDON, ENGLAND

"What happened?" Thurston asked.

"We ruffled a few feathers, and it would seem they didn't like it," Traynor replied.

"And they shot the shit out of the motel you were staying at."

"That's about it. They also took some casualties."

"Did you learn anything before this went down?"

"No."

"All right, sit tight. I'll see what MI5 can do for you."

"Thanks, ma'am."

The call disconnected. Thurston dialed the direct number she had for Fitzgerald. "We have a small problem in Northern Ireland."

"You'd better tell me about it."

After she finished, surprisingly, Fitzgerald chuckled. "You people sure know how to get a reaction."

"I suppose one good thing came from it. We have a good idea that the Finns are involved."

"How is your team in Libya doing?"

"They've tracked their target to what looks like a terrorist training camp in the desert."

"I guess that's that, then," the MI5 man said.

"Not hardly. They're about to go in and get him."

"I see. Good luck. I'll have someone take care of the Northern Ireland thing for you."

"Thank you."

———

BELFAST, NORTHERN IRELAND

"What kind of fucking gobshite are you?" Finn seethed at his son. "I told you to leave it alone, and now you've got four of my men killed. Not only that, you've given them what they wanted. Whoever they bloody are."

"But, Da!"

"Shut up, I'm thinking."

Silence descended on the living room. Finn's face moved through a range of expressions until it settled on one—a grim, determined look that brought a nod of satisfaction. "We check the shipment is right tomorrow, and then we leave for Nottinghamshire. Have Braden meet us at the estate. And let your sister know. I would like to see her when we arrive."

"Yes, sir."

"And don't fuck anything else up," Finn growled at his son. "The future of Ireland depends on what we're doing. Is there any word about Bob Murphy?"

"No, Da, he's disappeared."

"Probably best. Keep trying."

"Yes, Da."

His father left the living room and Kyran sat on the sofa, brooding over his father's treatment of him. After all, he was only trying to help. Couldn't his father see that? He took the cell from his pocket and dialed a familiar number. A sleepy voice answered. "Hello?"

"Hey, sis."

"Kyran?" Keira Finn said. "Do you have any idea what the time is?"

He could picture his sister, long dark hair mussed from sleep, tired eyes, pale skin, a picture of beauty closely resembling their mother, who had passed some years back from a brain aneurism. "Yeah, sorry. Da wanted me to call you. We're coming to the estate. He said he wants to see you."

"Couldn't it have waited until morning?"

"Sorry. I just wanted to hear your voice."

"You and Da been fighting again?"

"He doesn't understand me, Keira."

"Jesus, Kyran. Do we have to do this now? Wait until you get here, and then we'll talk. All right? I have an early shift at the hospital, and I need at least another hour of sleep."

"Okay. We'll talk then. Love you."

"Love you too. Bye."

The call disconnected, and Kyran put the cell back into his pocket. He stared at the flickering orange flames of the fire. He'd prove himself to his father somehow. Then he would *have* to be taken seriously.

———

LIBYA

The knife sliced across the terrorist's throat, and warm blood spurted. Kane let the man drop, wiped the blood off the blade, and replaced the knife in its sheath. He brought the M6 back up and proceeded to a stack of forty-four-gallon drums, where he took a knee. "Bring them up, Knocker."

"Roger."

Three more operators emerged from the darkness, while the fourth, Cara, remained on a small rise of land to the west, her L129 tucked into her shoulder as she watched their progress through the night-vision scope.

Knocker, Axe, and Brick joined Kane. "Knocker, Brick, take the radio bunker. Nothing gets out. We'll go after Kubar."

They split into two teams. Knocker and Brick worked their way through the dimly lit compound toward a structure surrounded by sandbags stacked four high. Inside it would be excavated out another four or five feet to help with the heat of the day.

Standing outside was a guard. The two team men stopped near a pile of ammunition crates. Between them and the commo bunker was perhaps twenty meters of open ground. Their chance of covering it without being seen was minimal since the guard was looking in their direction. They could shoot him, but any noise from this close would alert whoever was inside.

"Reaper Two," Knocker whispered into his comms. "The tango standing guard at the commo bunker. Put him to sleep."

"Sending."

The round streaked out of the darkness. The two operators heard it pass above them and then the low thud as the round impacted its target. The guard dropped where he stood. He'd no sooner hit the desert floor than the two men were up and moving, each covering their designated area on approach.

Knocker burst through the flap of canvas that acted as a door. The inside was dimly lit by a single bare bulb, the power provided by the generator behind the bunker. The radio operator inside spun in surprise. Knocker's M6 spat three shots, and the terrorist died before he could scream.

Brick joined him as Knocker said into his headset, "Commo bunker secured."

His comms came to life, but instead of Kane, it was Cara. "Reaper Three, kill the generator."

"Roger that."

They moved to the rear of the bunker, and Brick found the kill switch for the generator. The machine sputtered and died, and the few lights inside the camp perimeter dimmed and faded to black. Then they pulled down their NVGs and waited for the inevitable uproar and confusion.

Kane and Axe paused just long enough to fix their NVGs when the lights went out, then continued making their way toward the tented structure where they knew Kubar to be. Kane caught the first vestiges of movement to his left when a terrorist staggered out of a tent. The Team Reaper commander held his fire. He could see the man, but the man couldn't see him because he and Axe were sticking to the shadows.

They reached the structure, and Kane let the M6 hang by its strap. He took out his Glock and entered. Kubar was starting to stir. Kane planted a knee in the middle of the terrorist's chest and pressed the handgun against his forehead, hand clamped over his mouth. "Not a sound, asshole, or I'll scramble your brains good and proper."

Kane rolled him onto his front and zip-tied his wrists together. Then he dragged the terrorist to his feet. With a thick accent, Kubar hissed, "You will never get away."

"That would be bad for you."

"I am not afraid to die."

"I beg to differ. That's why you always send others to die for you. Move."

They retraced their steps outside, the terrorist boss leading the way. Figures were appearing all over the camp. "Reaper Two, sitrep? Over."

"You need to exfil to the south, Reaper."

"Roger."

"To me, Brothers! To me! The infidels are among us!"

"Son of a bitch" Kane growled and hit Kubar in the back of his head. It wasn't enough to knock the man out, but it stopped his yelling. "Cara, we're going to need the hand of God on this one. Reach out and touch them."

"Already on it, Reaper."

"Reaper Three and Five, regroup to the south side of the compound. Don't mess around."

"Coming your way, Reaper."

"Reaper One, sitrep, over."

It was Thurston. Obviously the ISR feed they were watching was causing some concern amongst those back in England.

"We've got Kubar, ma'am. Just extracting now."

"Good luck. We're seeing a lot of movement."

"You should be here," he said sarcastically before signing off.

Out of the darkness loomed three terrorists. Axe opened fire with the suppressed SAW, and the three bodies dropped in their tracks.

"This way," Kane said, pushing Kubar in front of him. "It's time to leave."

———

Cara changed out an empty magazine from the L129 and replaced it with a fresh twenty-round mag. She brought the weapon back into her shoulder and sought another target. The compound was starting to fill with flashes. She picked out Knocker and Brick moving between two tents, unaware of the three shooters on the other side coming their way. She sighted on the lead terrorist and squeezed the trigger. "Heads up, Reaper Three, tangos close."

She saw Knocker react, his movements quick as he turned and fired a steady stream of bullets at the two remaining shooters. They collapsed to the ground, and Knocker's voice came back through Cara's comms. "Thanks, Reaper Two."

The firing continued; the terrorists shot wildly at targets that weren't even there. The team used the confusion to exfil the camp with their prisoner and regroup outside the "wire".

From there, they circled back to the north and met up with Cara.

"Just another night, huh, Reaper?" Cara asked.

"Something like that. How's your ammo?"

"Two mags left. What about you and the others?"

"We'll get by if we don't get tangled in a firefight for too long."

"We'd better get out of here, then."

"Brick, you're on point. Axe, rear security."

Cara looked at Knocker. "How are your feet?"

"Still there, ma'am."

"Knocker." She stared at him, and although he couldn't see it, he felt it.

"They hurt like blazes, but I'll get by."

"Let me or Brick know if they get worse, all right?"

"Yes, ma'am."

The group started north, the chill of the desert night air more noticeable the closer it got to daybreak. Then to the east, the first light of dawn started to crest the horizon, orange fingers reaching out across the cloudless sky. Kane called a halt and checked his comms. "Bravo, copy?"

"I'm here, Reaper One." It was Ferrero.

"Zero, I estimate we're perhaps three klicks from the coast. Do we have a bird overhead yet?"

"Negative, Reaper. We're about ten minutes out from having eyes on you."

"Roger that. Reaper One, out."

"Reaper," Cara called to him from a low crest to their front.

He looked up at her. "What is it?"

"You'd better get up here."

He trudged past Knocker. "Keep an eye on Kubar."

"If he tries anything, I'll bury him where he sits."

Kane walked up the rise and knelt beside Cara. "What's up?"

"The highway. Look."

He stared across the desert, and in the orange light, he could see what concerned her. Police checkpoint. "Shit."

"That's not all." She pointed to the south. A pall of

dust hung in the air. "I'd say our friends have caught up to us."

———

"They've got us between a rock and a hard place," Kane said to the others. "I'm open to ideas."

"Dig in," said Axe.

"What if we try a ruse?" Knocker asked.

"I'm listening."

"We take up a position between the two forces and dig in. Once the jihadis crest the rise, Cara fires a shot at the police checkpoint. We get them shooting at each other."

"What kind of an idea is that?" Axe asked.

"One that has worked before, dog nuts."

"Yeah? When?"

"In World War Two. An allied force got stuck between two German forces. They tried it, and it worked."

"Uh-huh."

Cara leaned close to Knocker. "That was a movie. You know that, right?"

"It worked, though."

Cara rolled her eyes. "Dick."

"It's all we've got."

"Let's do it, then," Kane agreed, and ten minutes later, they had found a wash and taken cover.

Not long after, the terrorists appeared on the ridge. "All right, Cara, this is it. Do your thing."

The suppressed L129 nestled against her shoulder, and she fired at the checkpoint. She repeated the move twice more, deliberately missing. It wasn't long before the police had scattered and were firing at the terrorists along the low ridgeline.

For a plan that shouldn't have worked, it went well. Soon both sides were laying down heavy fire at each other. Kane said, "We'll use the wash. It looks like it leads to a culvert under the road. Come on, follow me."

They traversed the wash as bullets rattled around them. Knocker kept Kubar moving forward until they reached the culvert. The diameter was just large enough for them to crawl through. "Knocker, you first."

"Do we have to go through there, Reaper?" Axe asked. "You know there could be—"

"Don't fucking say it," Knocker snapped in a low voice. "Don't even think it. I'm the poor prick that has to go first."

"Better you than me," Axe grunted.

"Move it," Kane growled.

The Brit got down on his belly and started through the confined space. His boots were still visible when he froze.

Kane tapped his ankle. "Come on, keep going."

"I kind of have a problem," Knocker replied.

"You stuck?"

"Kinda."

"What do you mean?"

"If you'd be good enough to tell this cobra to fuck off, I'd be only too happy to keep going."

Axe looked at Kane, wide-eyed. "I told you, didn't I?"

"Shut up, Axe," Kane muttered. "Just shut the fuck up."

———

Knocker could feel the sweat rolling down his face and onto his chin, then dripping onto the dirt and sand of the culvert. He tried to remain calm but found it somewhat difficult while facing eight feet of death. He heard Kane's voice in his ear. "How close is it?"

"Close enough to give me a good old-fashioned tongue kiss."

The snake's hood flattened. One good thing about the confined space and probably the only good thing about the whole situation was that the cobra couldn't rise to full height. He just hoped it wasn't a spitter.

Meanwhile, outside in the wash amid the cacophony of the surrounding firefight, Kane and the others were desperately trying to figure out what they could do to help their comrade. "We could grab his ankles and drag him out as fast as we can," Axe suggested.

"Maybe," Kane said thoughtfully.

"If he gets bit while you're doing that," Brick said, "it'll most likely be neck or face. I can't help him. He'll die."

"What if I go over the top and distract it from the other side?" Cara suggested.

"The problem is getting over there without getting shot at. If they see you, it'll draw fire on us."

"What's more important?" Cara asked.

"There are no two ways. Get ready."

Cara climbed up the embankment and poised herself to break over the top. "Knocker, Cara is going to try and distract the snake so you can get out of there."

"Anytime now is good."

There was a scrabble of gravel, and Cara disappeared over the lip of the embankment. Keeping low, she ran as fast as she could across the two lanes of asphalt and slid down the other side to the mouth of the culvert.

She lowered herself to her stomach and squeezed into the opening, hoping the cobra didn't have any—

"Fuck."

CHAPTER 6

LIBYAN DESERT

CARA BACKED out slowly and leaned against the embankment. She pressed her talk button and said, "Reaper, we've got a slight problem."

"What is it?"

"A second snake at this end."

"You're shitting me?"

"Not today."

"All right, stay there. We'll have to go with the original plan and hope for the best. Knocker, did you get that?"

"Yeah, great fucking plan. I can see the headstone now. 'Here lies Raymond 'Knocker' Jensen. We hoped for the best'."

"Stop crying," Brick said. "What's the worst that could happen? The snake bites you, and the snake dies."

"Swap you places, cock."

"No, I'm claustrophobic."

"Fuck off."

"Cowboy up, sunshine."

"Shit, no. Argh—"

Knocker's legs started thrashing amid high-pitched shrieks. "Get him out," Kane barked.

The Team Reaper commander grabbed one foot, and Axe grabbed the other. The two men pulled hard, dragging the Brit free of the concrete tomb. As soon as Knocker was out, both men threw themselves away from the former SAS man. He wasn't the only one emerging from within. In the Brit's right hand was a writhing, angry eight-foot-long serpent that was trying its best to sink its fangs into flesh.

"Holy shit!" Axe exclaimed, backpedaling.

Kane was stunned, as was Brick. Knocker flung the hissing snake away in desperation, oblivious to the direction.

A cry of alarm emanated from Kubar's lips as the thick body of the beast wrapped around his throat. Before he could free himself from the serpent, it struck, its movements a blur to the naked eye. Fangs embedded deep in the terrorist's throat, pumping their lethal toxin into the flesh. "It bit me!" Knocker cried. "The fucking thing bit me!"

Brick jumped on him. "Keep still. Stop frigging moving. You'll only pump the venom further."

Knocker stopped. His eyes were filled with fear. "You got to help me, Brick."

"Where did it get you?"

"Here," Knocker said and lifted his chin to show Brick the flesh of his exposed throat and the two puncture wounds in it.

The former SEAL's mind reeled. What could he do

with that? They were in the desert, and he had no antivenin.

"Reaper, what's going on?" Cara asked impatiently.

"Wait one, Reaper Two."

"Brick, aren't you going to do something?" Knocker pleaded.

"There's nothing I can do, Ray."

The Brit gave a resigned chuckle. "You called me Ray. A sure sign I'm fucked."

"How do you feel?"

"Heart's racing. Sweating. Feel hot."

"Hey, look at Kubar," Axe blurted.

Kane and Brick turned their heads to look at the terrorist. He was lying on the ground, convulsing. "Damn it," Kane cursed and started toward the man.

Brick grabbed him by the arm. "Stop."

"What?"

"The cobra."

Kane saw the snake slithering away from the terrorist and paused. Once he figured it was far enough away, he hurried to Kubar's side.

The puncture wounds in the flesh of the man's throat were clear to see, with thin lines of blood running out of them. It only took one look to tell the terrorist was dying.

"He's done for," Kane called over his shoulder. Then he looked at Knocker, who'd also been bitten on the throat. "Brick, how is he?"

The former SEAL frowned. "He looks surprisingly fine."

Kane moved to the Brit's side. "Knocker, how are you feeling?"

He looked at the dead terrorist. "Better than him."

The Team Reaper commander glanced at his medic. "What do you think?"

Brick shrugged. "Dry bite? I've heard of them."

"What do you mean?"

"The snake bites but doesn't inject any venom."

"You mean he'll be all right?" Kane asked.

"Looks like it."

Kane looked at Knocker. "Get up, you git. We need to keep moving."

"But I got bit by the snake."

"You'll be fine. Now, get up."

"I'd hate to be you," Brick said to Kane.

"Why?"

"You've got to tell Thurston you lost her HVT from snakebite."

"Yeah. Maybe that can wait."

The team prepared to cross the road. The firing between the two parties could still be heard, although it sounded like it was ebbing.

"Once we get across this, we're on the stretch to the coast. Let's move."

They crossed the road one at a time, none of them drawing any fire. Once they were all on the other side, Kane pointed them toward the coast and their date with the RHIB.

———

LONDON, ENGLAND

"Shit! Fuck!" Thurston exclaimed, throwing a pen across the room. "How the hell does this happen?"

"It did. That's all I know," Ferrero said.

"So, we're back in the same place as when we first started."

"Slick has been doing some digging, and he found out Finn has an estate in Nottinghamshire where his daughter lives. We know he's up to something. Maybe we can find out from his daughter."

"How?"

"We could put someone close to her."

"You mean undercover?"

Ferrero nodded. "Yes."

"I'll think about it. Tell me about his daughter."

"She works at the local hospital in the town where she lives. She's a triage nurse. Used to be a medic in the 3rd Infantry Battalion in the 1st Irish Brigade. Served in the Congo, Liberia, Lebanon."

"Is there anything tying her to any of the IRA factions?"

Ferrero shook his head. "Not that we can see. That doesn't mean it's not there."

"Any lover, boyfriend, husband, kids?" Thurston asked.

"No. I can have Slick do you up a dossier if you like?"

"Yes, all right. We'll do that."

"I'll have it on your desk as soon as I can."

"Before you go," Thurston said, "did the team get picked up all right?"

"Yes, ma'am. They're headed home."

Thurston snorted. "Home. What is home these days?"

"I guess it's where we are, Mary. We're all family."

"Yes, I suppose you're right. But I feel like I've

taken the team down a hole from which there is no coming back."

"Have you talked to Hank Jones?"

She waved the question away. "He's too busy."

"Talk to him, Mary. He'll listen."

"Maybe you're right."

"I'll get the folder on Finn's daughter for you."

"Thanks, Luis."

"Any time."

———

BELFAST, NORTHERN IRELAND

The salt air came in off the Irish Sea, carrying with it the scent of fish and rotting seaweed. Finn and his small entourage waited patiently for the forklift to put the salt-rusted shipping container down so it could be opened. Black diesel smoke belched from the exhaust of the orange machine as it reversed and then moved forward. Two of Finn's bodyguards stood off to the side. Hidden under their long coats were MAC-10 submachine guns. Even Kyran was armed with a Beretta in a shoulder holster out of sight.

The shipping container was placed on the concrete pad, and the forklift was turned off. In the brief silence that followed, the cries of gulls and other sea birds could be heard. In the distance, a ship's horn emitted a deep groan.

"Get that thing open," Finn ordered.

A dry screech sounded as the handles were turned and the right-side door swung open. It protested with a loud grinding sound, exposing a wall of cardboard boxes. "Move them," Finn ordered.

Two men stepped forward and removed the false wall. Finn, Kyran, and another man stepped inside, where three wooden crates were lying longways on the floor. The lid came free of the first crate, exposing a dozen AK-74s, the same number of MP-443 Grach handguns, and two RPG-26 disposable launchers.

"The other crates?" Finn asked.

"Ammunition and plastic explosives, along with vests for the men," Kyran replied.

"Yuri has done well."

"Yes, he asked well for them too."

Finn turned to the man beside him. "When will they arrive in Scotland?"

"Tomorrow. From there, they will be loaded straight onto a lorry and shipped south to your estate."

"I don't want anything to go wrong, Ardan," Finn said sternly. "They need to be there on time."

"I will be with them," the red-haired man replied. "Everything will be fine."

He seemed satisfied with that, but everyone there knew what would happen if things went wrong. The old man wasn't one to suffer failure lightly.

Finn's cell phone rang. He answered it and walked away from the group to where he could talk without being overheard. Kyran frowned and turned to Ardan. "Close the lid and lock it up."

No sooner had Kyran walked outside when he felt a cold, hard gun barrel pressed against his forehead. "You fucking gobshite lying son of a motherless leprechaun."

"Whoa, wait! What did I do?"

"I hate failure, but you know how much more I hate liars? Get on your knees, boy."

"Da, wait."

"You told me Bob disappeared—"

"He has, Da," Kyran blurted.

"He disappeared because he's in a fucking London morgue, asshole," Finn roared.

"I tried to stop it, Da, honest. But I was too late. Braden had already done it."

"So then you lied to me instead of owning up to it like a man," Finn snarled, spittle flying from his lips. "Your sister has more balls than you do. She should have been the boy and you the sissy."

"Da, don't, please."

Finn walked around behind his son and placed the barrel against the back of his head. The hammer came back, and Kyran whimpered, "Da, please."

"You killed my friend."

"Da—"

The flat report rattled off the surrounding shipping containers, making those nearby jump. "Get up," Finn hissed.

Kyran staggered to his feet and looked at his father. "Da."

"Just shut up and get in the car."

Kyran turned away quickly and walked toward the vehicle, then opened the door and got inside. Finn turned to Ardan. "I will see you at the estate."

"Sure thing, boss."

Finn followed his son to the vehicle and climbed in. Kyran sat in the back, his gaze focused out the tinted window. Finn thought about saying something before discarding the idea. Let him stew for a while.

The old man looked down at his trembling hands, knowing how close he had come to putting his son in the ground. Hell, he still might yet.

The driver climbed in beside him and looked at his boss. Finn nodded. "Take us to the plane, Connor."

"Yes, sir."

————

FINN ESTATE, NOTTINGHAMSHIRE

"Hello, Da," Keira Finn said to her father, planting a kiss on his leathery cheek.

"Hello, baby. You're looking thin. Are you eating?"

"Stop it," she replied to his question. "You fuss too much."

"Is Braden here?"

"Yes."

"Good." He stepped back to examine his daughter more closely. Her dark hair had been allowed to grow longer than he remembered. Her skin was still pale, and her eyes sparkling. "You're your mother reincarnated, lass."

She smiled and looked at her brother. He seemed more cowed than usual, which set alarm bells off in her head. She put her arms around her brother and whispered in his ear, "Are you all right, Kyran?"

"I'm fine," he replied loud enough for his father to hear.

The old man snorted. "Of course, he's fucking fine. Why wouldn't he be? Bob Murphy? Now that's another issue right there."

Keira could see the fire in her father's eyes, but that didn't deter her. "Leave him alone, Da."

"Leave him alone?" he asked, perplexed. "Do you want to know what the little shite did?"

"No, Da, I don't. I don't even want to know why you and your men are here."

"It's my place, and I'll visit if I want to."

"Whatever, Da. Just leave Kyran alone."

"If he expects to be head of this family one day, then the boy needs to learn how to become a man, not the sniveling wretch that he is. Maybe you should become the man of the family?"

"Not likely. I'm happy doing what I do."

"And what about your country, girl? What about the cause?"

"Your cause, Da, not mine."

"Wash your filthy mouth out."

"Fuck you, Da. Fuck you."

"What did you say?" His voice was low and menacing.

"You heard me. I did my time for my country. Congo, Liberia, and other shithole places I saw men and women die in. But not innocents, Da."

"They're casualties of war, Keira," Finn snapped at his daughter.

"Your war, Da. Not mine. Murder is what it is."

"Hush your mouth, girl."

"I spend my time saving lives, not taking them. I'll be gone by the end of the day. I'll not stay here with you."

Keira turned to leave. "Keira, wait, please."

She stopped and turned back to her father. His face had softened. "Please don't go. Stay with me. At least tonight, and if you want to leave tomorrow, I won't stop you."

"What about Kyran?"

"What about him?" Finn asked, eyes narrowing.

"Da—"

"All right, I'll take it easy on him if it'll keep you off my back."

"How long are you here for?"

His reply was interrupted by the arrival of a lorry that made its way along the wide gravel driveway. Keira frowned. "What's this?"

"Nothing you need to worry about. Kyran, tell him to park it in the barn."

"Da—" Keira started.

"You made it quite clear you didn't want to know, Keira. Leave it at that."

"Mother of God," she breathed.

———

LONDON, ENGLAND

Fitzgerald listened to the proposal, but he was apprehensive about the idea. He winced, shook his head, and said, "I don't like it, Mary. It's risky. Finn isn't a very trusting man. We tried to get two operatives inside his organization before, but both disappeared."

Thurston frowned. "You mean you've been watching him, and he was still able to pull this thing off?"

"Not our finest hour, I'll admit."

"Were you able to find out anything?"

"No. When I heard you were coming over, I put

this together. It's probably stuff you already know, but there might be something in there you can use." He handed her a folder.

She opened it, and the first thing she saw was a picture of a dark-haired woman in a hospital uniform. "Is this the daughter?"

"Yes. She works at Newark Hospital."

"Is it up to date?"

"Taken last week."

"It's better than the one we have."

"She lives on the Finn estate."

"Do you have it under surveillance?"

"Not anymore. Everything was pulled off it to concentrate on the terror threat."

"They're looking the wrong way."

"Yes, I agree. But my hands are tied."

Thurston flipped the photo and found another.

Fitzgerald said, "Kyran Finn. Timid, meek, scared, and the deadliest of the lot. He'll do anything to please his father. The thing is his father hates the boy. Thinks him a stain on society and the family name."

"Do you have anything on the hired help?"

"Next picture. Braden O'Connor."

Thurston was looking at a picture of a solidly built man with brown hair. He had a rugged face that might be considered handsome if it weren't for his eyes. They were cold, bottomless pits of anger.

Fitzgerald continued. "He's Finn's enforcer. We think—I say think, but it's more than likely true—that he was responsible for at least fourteen deaths in the past two years."

Thurston looked at the MI5 boss. "Why would Finn kill his friend?"

Fitzgerald spread his hands. "No idea. It doesn't make sense. They go back a long way."

"Any sign of the fourth lorry?"

"I was going to ask you the same thing."

"I guess we're both out of luck. Once my team gets back, I'll put the op in motion. It's the only way we'll have any chance of finding out what their plans are."

"Good luck, Mary. Keep me updated."

CHAPTER 7

LONDON, ENGLAND

"GATHER AROUND, people. We've got a mission to prepare for." Thurston waited patiently until everyone was seated before continuing. A picture of Keira Finn appeared on a screen to the right of the general's position. "Keira Finn. She is the target. We're going to try to use her to get inside her father's organization."

"How are we going to do that?" Knocker asked.

"I need someone to volunteer to get shot."

"Don't look at me," the Brit said. "I already got bit by a snake, thanks to dickhead beside me."

"How am I to blame?" Axe asked, not needing to feign being hurt by the remark.

"You were the one who said it."

"No, I didn't."

"You thought it."

"No—"

"You kind of did," said Cara.

Axe smiled. "I did, didn't I?"

"Uh-huh."

"You done?" Thurston asked.

"Yes, ma'am," Axe replied.

"It's decided, then. Knocker gets shot."

"Fuck me."

"It makes sense. No American is going to try to kidnap her off the street, are they?" Thurston pointed out.

"Snakebit and shot in the same week. Next I'll be blown up."

"I might be able to help with that," Thurston said drily. "Reaper will be put inside if possible and see what information he can get if any."

"Are we getting desperate, ma'am?" Kane asked.

"You could say that. She's a triage nurse at Newark Hospital. We'll stage an attempted kidnapping; you rescue her. You'll be wired—"

"Not a good idea, ma'am."

"Don't worry, Reaper," Slick said. "The new toys I have, someone could search you and they still couldn't find it."

"All right, then."

"Cara and Knocker will run surveillance. Brick, Axe, you'll be backup. Only if required. We don't know anything about her, and she could be daddy's girl and quite dangerous. After all, she's served in more than one war zone."

The picture on the screen changed; the one of the girl disappeared. "This is her home."

They all studied it. The house was a stone mansion. Ivy climbing the left half of the front wall, and it was two stories tall. "These pictures came from the Security Services."

More pictures appeared, including one of a barn that was almost as big as the house.

"We're still trying to figure out who killed Bob Murphy."

"It wasn't Finn?" Cara asked.

"I talked to Fitzgerald, and we're of the same opinion. Why would the man kill his best friend?"

"They could have had a falling out," Axe put forward.

"True, but highly unlikely."

"Next is this guy." Another picture. "Braden O'Connor. Finn's enforcer. We know he's in the country because Slick managed to pull his picture at a train station time-stamped the day of the bombing."

Kane said, "How far is it from the hotel to the train station?"

Thurston looked at Swift. "Slick?"

He glanced at his tablet and let his fingers dance across the touch screen. "Five miles."

"See if you can find him within a few blocks of the hotel and match it up with the time. He could well be our killer."

"If he is, it doesn't gel with the theory that Finn didn't kill his best friend," Ferrero said.

"Let's just see what happens, and we'll follow that rabbit then. In the meantime, we still need to find that fourth lorry. Troy, Pete, that'll fall to you."

"Where are we supposed to start on that?" Troy asked.

Thurston smiled. "You're smart. I'm sure you'll think of something."

Swift said, "I've been running a new algorithm for the past few days. If it pops up, it'll let me know."

"All right, that's all for the moment. I'll get copies of this folder to you within the hour. Field team, get ready to head to Nottinghamshire. You leave tomorrow."

———

Cara lay with her head on Kane's chest. "I think the general is feeling responsible for us being here and not back home," she said.

Kane sighed. "Maybe, but it's not her fault. How's Jimmy getting on?"

"He started school in Hereford while we were downrange."

"How did it go?"

"Great. He sounds happy. His accent makes him the most popular kid in his class, and the girls are already asking him out."

"Cool."

"But get this. Guess who took him on the first day?"

Kane shrugged. "The people looking after him?"

"Hank Jones."

There was no disguising the surprise in Kane's voice. "The general?"

"Yes. I called to thank him, and he said, 'Us guys have got to stick together.'"

"He'll have him in uniform before long," Kane said with a chuckle.

She punched him in the ribs. "Not funny."

"Ow. You don't want him to follow in your footsteps?"

"No. Not seeing the things we see. Doing what we do. I want him to stay sweet and innocent."

"You realize that if it's what he wants to do—"

"Yes, I know. But I can still try to dissuade him."

"If he's anything like his mother, it'll be like a duck to water."

"That's what worries me." She looked at Kane. "Maybe you could talk to him. Steer him away from any such thoughts."

"This is something for you and him," Kane said to her.

For a moment she tensed, and he thought she was going to get angry with him. Instead, she relaxed and said, "You're right."

As she climbed out of bed, Kane asked, "Where are you going?"

"Back to my room."

"Why?"

"If I stay here, I'm not going to get any sleep. From here on out, I'm going to need to be at the top of my game, just like you." She leaned over and kissed him. "Later."

She got dressed and left. Kane was almost asleep when the phone rang. He looked at the number and hit a key. "Doc?"

"John, sorry it's late, but...Melanie, John. It's Melanie."

"What is it, Doc?" he asked anxiously.

"She's awake."

———

After all this time. All these years. He could hardly believe it. Mel, awake.[1] After he hung up, he couldn't sleep. Hashing over and trying to make sense of everything David "Doc" Harper had told him kept him from the Land of Nod. Melanie had awoken two days ago. At first, the medical staff hadn't been sure what it meant, but she'd remained awake for long periods, slept for a while, and then woken once more. She was still a long way from being herself again and would require months of therapy, but Harper had said the prognosis was good.

"Would you like to talk to her?" Harper had asked.

Kane had answered the question three times. The first two, he couldn't get his voice past his lips. "Sure, Doc."

"Hello?" The voice was dry and raspy.

"Mel?"

"John?"

"Oh, dear God, it's good to hear your voice," he said hoarsely. "So good. How are you feeling?"

"Tired."

Kane smiled. Then he remembered his parents. "Mel, Ma and Pa..."

"I know, Johnny. The doctor told me," she said quietly.

"I'll get on the next plane, Mel. I'll come see you."

"No. You can't. The one thing...the one thing I've —" She coughed. "The doctor told me what has been happening. About you. You can't come. I'm fine."

"Just as soon as you're well enough, Mel, I'm getting you out of there."

"Okay, Johnny. Okay."

"I've missed you, kiddo."

"Not much of a kid anymore."

"Love you, Mel."

"Love you too."

He'd talked to Harper for a while after that, then the call had ended. Now he sat waiting for Thurston and Ferrero. When they appeared in the doorway, he jumped to his feet. Ferrero took one look at him and said, "It's Melanie, isn't it?" He knew that the only thing that put Kane so visibly on edge was his sister.

"She's awake."

"Good Lord," Ferrero murmured. "After all this time."

"That's wonderful news, Reaper," Thurston said.

"It is, but I can't see her. I talked to her, but I can't get back to the States—" He broke off, tears welling in his eyes.

"Once she's well enough, we'll get her over here," Thurston told him. "All right?"

He nodded. "I was hoping you would say that."

"Don't worry, Reaper. When the time comes, I'll have it all organized for you."

"Thank you."

"All right. Now I need your head in the game."

"You got it."

————

NEWARK, NOTTINGHAMSHIRE

It felt like one of those eighties movies where they were on a stakeout in a delivery van. It had all the modern gadgets, but they couldn't help but have that lame feeling. Outside it was dark, the night lit only by a couple of spaced-out streetlamps. Kane was dressed in jeans and a T-shirt, over which he wore a leather jacket. Cara was dressed pretty much the same way. Knocker, on the other hand, was dressed in black and had a ski mask on his head.

Tucked into the back of Kane's pants was his Glock, its magazine loaded with blanks. That was the only one, though. The two magazines he had in his pockets were the real deal.

Knocker adjusted the special vest beneath his shirt. "All right, I'm ready to go. We just need our lady in waiting."

Kane grinned wickedly. Knocker didn't like it. "You sure you've got the right mag in that thing in your pants?"

"It's the right one," Cara said with a smile.

"I'm not talking about his dobber."

"I know."

Another thirty minutes passed while they sat, the weather closing in the longer they waited. Scudding showers, cold, and the wind. Typical British weather. Cara looked at her watch. "Time to go to work."

"Typical," Knocker growled. "Wait until it's pissing down rain, and then it's time to go."

Kane slapped him on the back. "Buck up."

They stepped out of the van and into the rainy night. The wind whipped their clothes, and for the first time, Kane realized how bitter the British weather could be. The pair separated, both on comms, with Cara in the van. They took up their positions and then waited once more.

———

Keira Finn exited the hospital and walked into the breathtaking chill. "Mother of God," she growled. When she'd arrived at work earlier in the day, it had been rather pleasant. Now, quite frankly, the weather was shit.

Her hair was tied back in a ponytail, and she pulled her coat up over her head to try to keep some of the drizzle off her. As she hurried across the driveway to the parking lot, her soft-soled shoe splashed into a puddle, causing her foot to become wet. "Bastard."

Once across the drive, she walked through an opening in the low hedge. On the other side was a black BMW, most likely a doctor's ride. She passed the rear fender and took another step, and the man seemed to materialize in front of her, ski mask pulled down and a gun in his hand. "Not so fast, Princess."

Keira stopped suddenly, but instead of fear on her face, Knocker saw that she was assessing the situation—her military training. He needed to do something to put her off-guard. He moved toward her, weapon raised, and shouted, "Get on the ground!"

Instead of obeying, she did something unexpected. She tried to disarm him.

The cow had balls; he had to give her that. In another time and place, he might even like her. Just not now. His left hand shot out, bunched in a fist, and clipped her on the jaw, stunning her. She staggered and sank to her knees.

"Take after your da, huh?" Knocker growled. "It's going to be fun to do this to you. Just think about your da while I do it."

Knocker grabbed her by the hair and dragged her to her feet. "Let's go somewhere a little more private."

"Hey, what are you doing?"

"Fuck." Knocker spun, his weapon in the firing position.

Two shots rang out, and Knocker dropped to the wet asphalt of the parking lot. Keira was still stunned but was fighting her way to her feet. Kane approached her, his weapon pointed at Knocker, who lay prone at his feet. "Are you alright?" he asked her.

"What?" Keira asked as she swayed.

Kane grabbed her arm. "Hey, take it easy."

She looked at Knocker lying there, unmoving. "Oh, my. We have to help him."

"He's dead. We need to get out of here."

"No, I'm a nurse. I can help."

"He's dead."

"How do you know?"

"There wasn't time not to kill him. Listen, where's your ride?"

Keira was still confused. She waved at the other side of the lot. "Over there."

"Come on."

"Who are you?"

"I'll tell you soon," Kane replied impatiently. "But right now, we need to leave."

"I can't leave the scene of a crime."

"Listen, I just shot a guy who was trying to do God only knows what to you. I've got an illegal firearm, and the police are going to crucify me."

"No."

"Fine, I'm out of here." Kane started to walk away.

"Wait," Keira said. "Come with me."

They hurried across the lot to a red Peugeot. Keira opened the door on the driver's side. Kane asked, "Do you think you should drive?"

"I'm fine." She swayed.

"No, you're not." He hurried to the other side of the car. "Give me the keys."

Keira passed them over and walked to the passenger side, not letting go of the Peugeot.

They climbed in, and Kane started the vehicle. He selected reverse with the automatic shift. Thirty seconds later, they were driving out of the lot.

———

"The lady has got some brass; I'll give her that," Knocker said as he climbed into the rear of the van. "She's got the Irish blood coursing through her veins."

"Are you alright?" Cara asked without making a fuss.

"Sure. Didn't like giving her that love tap, though."

"It's what we do." He took off his shirt and vest, threw them in a corner, and removed his pants. The original reason for the clean clothes was the blood splatter. Being wet was a bonus. He put on dry clothes and asked, "Are we going?"

"Yes."

"Bravo, copy?" Cara said into her comms.

"Read you Lima Charlie, Reaper Two."

"Reaper One is in play, following now."

"Roger that. Keep us updated. Bravo out."

———

LONDON, ENGLAND

Troy and Traynor had gotten lucky. They had a lead on the lorry they were looking for. A report had come into the Security Services about a lorry appearing in a warehouse on the Thames.

Like most calls that came into the Met, it was anonymous. At the mention of a lorry, the call was quickly rerouted to MI5, who in turn passed it on to Thurston. It was then passed to her two operators. "Be careful. It's only a recon operation to make sure it's what we're looking for."

"Yes, ma'am." They left it at that.

It was a prick of a night, wet, cold, and pissing down rain. Great weather for operations, even better for ducks. Weapons drawn, they splashed through puddles toward the large warehouse. There was a light on inside, which meant someone was there.

They worked their way around to the rear of the building—in this case, the river side. Finding an unlocked door, they entered.

The interior of the building was filled with old equipment and wooden crates and pallets, which gave the pair plenty of cover. Well, it was supposed to.

The lorry was there all right. So were six armed men—that they could see. They found out the reality a little while later as they were leaving.

"There it is," Traynor said. "The thing is, what do they want with it?"

"Let's get some footage and get out of here," Troy replied.

He grabbed his cell and took some pictures of the lorry and the men. They were all armed with automatic weapons and looked as though they were preparing it for something. "There's no sign of explosives," Traynor said. "Not unless they're already in the back of the thing."

"We've got what we need," said Troy. "Let's get out of here."

They began their exfil and Traynor knocked over an empty oil drum—just one of those things that happens when you're trying to be quiet. The sound echoed throughout the warehouse, raising the alarm. Shouts rang out, and Troy looked at Traynor and shook his head. "That fucked that."

"Not my fault."

"Yeah," Troy replied, taking out his Glock. "Tell that to the man at the Pearly Gates when we get there."

A shooter appeared and opened fire with his automatic weapon. Troy fired twice while bullets ricocheted around him and dropped the man where he stood. The void was filled by a second man; this one, Traynor sent to meet St. Peter.

"Come on, let's get out of here," Troy growled, firing at a third man.

Shouts could be heard from their right. "There's more of them," Traynor said.

"Fantastic."

The air was suddenly filled with bullets. Troy and Traynor dived behind some wooden crates, which splintered when slugs tore into them. "Bravo, copy?" Troy shouted.

Ferrero's voice came on the comms. "Read you Lima Charlie. What's—"

"We've got a bit of a problem. We're pinned down by around a dozen shooters in the...in the warehouse. Shit. They've got automatic weapons, and we've got peashooters."

"Hang in there. Help is on the way. Out."

Traynor tapped Troy on the shoulder and pointed

at some forty-four-gallon drums near the far wall. "What do you think?"

"Shoot them and find out."

He did. Traynor raised his Glock and fired three times. Two of the drums sprang leaks, and fluid began pouring across the warehouse floor. "Well, you can shoot straight," Troy commented.

"Screw you," Traynor replied. "I wonder how flammable it is."

"Wait—" More bullets cracked close. "Wait until it gets to that metal stand there, and then we'll find out."

Troy fired five more rounds at a shooter before having to reload. He dropped out his magazine and replaced it with a fresh one, then glanced at the liquid as it streamed across the concrete, the thin rivulet like a long bony finger. When it reached the metal stand, he said, "Let's find out now."

Troy sighted on the stand and fired three shots. The first missed and the second hit, but nothing happened. The third hit as well, but this time a spark flashed when the round made contact. Not much, but enough to ignite the liquid. The pair watched as the flame turned from orange to blue and began to speed back toward the drums along the path the liquid had taken.

"Oh, shit, that's not a good sign," Traynor said hurriedly.

Troy was running by the time the last words passed his lips. "You're right. Move!"

The firing ceased abruptly. Then came the shouts. Panicked this time, not like before. Obviously, they'd seen the flames too.

By the time Troy and Traynor got to the door they had entered by, the fire had reached the drums. As they

passed through the doorway, the orange and black fireball from the explosion within was hot on their heels.

The noise was deafening, the heat from the blast
almost suffocating. They dove to the asphalt outside as
the wave washed over them.

"Shit," Traynor yelped.

The noise subsided, and Troy looked at the warehouse. It was on fire and starting to collapse, partially
destroyed by the blast. He looked at Traynor. "Oops."

———

NOTTINGHAMSHIRE, ENGLAND

Kane and Keira put Newark behind them, the wipers
swiping rhythmically across the windshield. The rain
was starting to ease, and the road became more visible,
although the reflection of the headlights still made it
difficult. Hedges sprang up on either side of the road,
thick growths that acted as fences.

"How much farther?" Kane asked.

"Another couple of miles, and then you need to
turn right."

Kane nodded and kept his concentration on the
road.

"Why?" Keira asked.

"Why what?"

"Why did you help me?"

"I saw you were in trouble and thought you could
use it."

"Why the gun?"

"I know some bad people, and they don't like me,"
he replied. "Be safer back in Afghan."

"You served?"

"Sure did. Couple of tours in Afghanistan, plus a few other places in between."

"Me too."

"You were in Afghanistan?" Kane asked, feigning surprise.

Keira shook her head and immediately regretted it. "No. Congo, Liberia, a few other places in Africa. I was a medic."

"Small world."

They reached the turn, and Kane signaled before taking it. The road narrowed even more than the last one. He said, "Don't they like roads in this country? Maybe they have a shortage of asphalt."

Keira chuckled. "You know what? I don't even know your name."

"John Kane," he replied.

"Pleased to meet you, John Kane. My name is Keira Walsh."

The surname caught him off-guard. A voice in his ear said, "That was her mother's maiden name."

"Pleased to meet you too, Keira Walsh. I take it from your accent that you're Irish?"

"It wasn't that hard to guess, was it?" she asked. "Just like you're from America."

"That was easier to pick out than your Irish accent," Kane said.

"No, you could have been from Canada."

"All right, you got me there."

"Turn up here," Keira said.

Kane slowed the vehicle and signaled to turn again. This time, however, he was met by wrought iron gates. "How do I get in?"

Keira reached into the glove compartment and found a small remote. She pressed the button, and the gates slowly opened. Kane drove through, and the gates automatically closed behind them. "I'm starting to feel out of place."

"It's all right, although I must warn you about my father and brother. They can be a little overprotective at times."

Kane's mind whirled. Finn and his son, here? This was unexpected. Ferrero said, "Just roll with it, Reaper. Cara and Knocker are only a few minutes behind you. This might be the opening you need."

"I didn't mean to scare you," Keira told him.

"Huh?"

"My father and brother. You went quiet suddenly."

"Oh, I'm fine. Just not used to meeting the family on the first date."

Soft laughter escaped her lips, then she winced. "Don't make me laugh. It hurts."

The Peugeot pulled into the turnaround in front of the house. It was bigger than Kane had thought. He turned the vehicle off and looked at his passenger. "Here we are."

"I'll see if someone will drive you back to Newark."

"I'm not sure if—" The door beside him opened, and cool air rushed in.

A handgun appeared in front of Kane's face, and a voice snarled, "Get out of the fucking car before I shoot you in the head."

---

1. See *Retribution*

CHAPTER 8

FINN ESTATE, NOTTINGHAMSHIRE

"KYRAN, WAIT!" Keira exclaimed.

Kane's movements were sudden and violent. He grabbed the barrel of the handgun and turned it savagely, almost breaking Kyran's finger. The Irishman cried out in pain and alarm. Before he knew what was happening, he was staring into the muzzle of his own weapon. "You shouldn't play with dangerous toys," Kane warned him.

"Kyran, you're a fucking moron," Keira told him. "Idiot."

"Who is he, Keira?"

"None of your business, now piss off."

Kyran held out his hand. "Give me my gun back."

"If you can't keep hold of it, you don't deserve to have one," Kane replied.

"What the hell is going on here?" Brian Finn snarled as he emerged from the house. While their attention was diverted, Kane took his earwig out and put it in his hand.

"Kyran is being a dick," Keira snapped as she climbed out of the Peugeot.

"What else is new?"

Kane got out, and the older Finn's eyes narrowed suspiciously. "Who is he?"

"Someone who helped me. Can we go inside now?" She looked at her father defiantly.

He nodded. "All right, but I'll be watching him."

"Oh, for fuck's sake."

While their attention was focused on Keira, Kane flicked the tiny earwig into a small bush beside the turnaround.

As they walked past Finn, Kane passed Kyran's weapon to him. "Children shouldn't be allowed to play with guns."

The young man glared at him.

Inside, the house was warm and dry, and Kane was shown to the large living room. A roaring fire was burning, and the room had a faint odor of woodsmoke. The fireplace surround was decorated with ornate marble carvings.

Kane stood near it to dry out a little. Keira excused herself while she changed. That left Kane in the room with her father and brother. Not long after, another man joined them. Braden O'Connor.

"How do you know my daughter?" Finn asked him.

"I met her tonight."

"Where?"

"In a parking lot."

"What were you doing there?" Kyran asked.

Kane stared at him. "Minding my own business."

"All right, Kyran," Finn said softly, "I'll ask the questions."

There was anger in the younger Finn's eyes, and Kane filed it away for later use. Finn said, "What were you doing in the car park?"

"Rescuing me from an attacker, if you must know," Keira said as she reentered the living room.

"What bastard attacker?" Finn growled. "I'll cut his fucking heart out."

"You won't have to worry about that. John shot him dead."

"Did he now?" Finn said and nodded at O'Connor.

The enforcer stepped forward. He drew his weapon and pointed it at Kane. The Team Reaper commander raised his hands. "Easy, buddy. All you have to do is ask. It's tucked down the back of my pants."

He turned so O'Connor could access it easily. Kane felt it being removed and turned back. The enforcer dropped the magazine and ejected the round in the chamber, then put the gun on the coffee table in the middle of the room.

"Is this really necessary?" Keira asked.

"What do you need a gun for, John? Is that right? John?"

Kane nodded. "That's right."

Finn spread his hands. "Well? Why?"

"In case I meet people like you." Kane kept his face passive, waiting for a reaction.

Finn's expression was uncertain. Then he smiled. "I like you. Now, answer the question."

"I rub people the wrong way. Some of them aren't so nice, so I carry a gun."

"What people?"

"Willy Pete."

"Willy Pete?" Finn asked.

"Yes."

The Irishman's face turned to granite. "Willy Pete is dead. Shot two nights ago."

"Yes, he was."

"You did it?"

"It seemed like the right choice at the time."

Willy Pete had indeed been shot two nights before in a deal gone bad between two of London's lesser-known crime lords. A firefight had broken out when the second party, Frankie Tyler, had tried to take the money as well the drugs. It was sloppy, and when the firing stopped, everyone was down. It gave Kane the perfect back story.

"Tell me about it."

"The official story was everyone was killed, shot by each other. What they didn't say was that one person got away. I was hired muscle for Frankie Tyler. Now I'm looking for new employment if I don't get killed beforehand."

"I have contacts. You know I can check your bull-shit story."

Kane looked him straight in the eye. "I don't give a fuck what you do. I did what I set out to, and now I'll leave." He started toward the table to get his weapon.

Out of the corner of his eye, he saw O'Connor move. He straightened and looked at the enforcer. "Do you think you can get that gun of yours out before I break your neck, asshole?"

"This is just great," Keira snapped. "The guy saves me from one of your enemies and—"

"Wait," Finn interrupted. "One of my enemies?"

"Yes, the man used your name. He knew who I was. He said something about making an example or something. Maybe I just should have gone to the police."

"The last thing we need is coppers crawling around the place," Kyran protested.

"Shut your gob," Finn hissed. He looked at Kane. "If you want work, I might be able to find you something. If you're interested?"

Kane shrugged. "Sure. Got nowhere else to be."

A cell in Finn's pocket rang. He answered it and listened. Kane watched the color and expression of his face change. The call disconnected, and he got to his feet. With a nod to his son and O'Connor, he said, "You'll have to excuse me. Business."

After they'd left the room, Kane picked up his weapon. Keira looked at him. "I'll find you a room if you like?"

Kane nodded and asked, "What is it that your father does?"

"You don't want to know."

"I guess if I'm going to work for him, I should know."

"I'd advise you to leave and not look back, but I figure you're a man who does as he pleases anyway, so I won't bother."

"Can't be any worse than what I was just doing."

She sighed. "You'd be surprised."

———

The following morning, the rain had gone but had left a leaden sky in its wake. Kane slept well, and when he showed up for breakfast the following morning, he found that Keira had cooked him a plate of bacon and eggs and tomatoes. "Looks good, thank you," he said as she placed it in front of him.

"I figure it's the least I could do after what you did last night," she said.

"You don't seem to be too troubled about it," Kane noted.

"I try not to be. If I were, I'd be a wreck. Besides, I have experience with it, remember?"

"True."

Kyran appeared and glared at Kane, obviously still smarting about what had happened the previous evening. He looked at his sister. "Where's mine?"

"Your what?"

"Breakfast."

"Get your own," she replied. "You're not useless."

"How come he gets his handed to him?" he asked churlishly.

"Grow up, Kyran."

He muttered something under his breath and walked over to the counter where the coffee pot was brewing.

Next to enter was Finn, and he looked about as happy as he had the night before. "I have a job for you this morning," he said to Kane. "I want you to go with Kyran and watch his back while he sees to a matter."

Kyran stared at his father.

"You have a problem, boy?"

"For God's sake, don't start at this time of the morning," Keira growled.

"He's got to learn to accept orders, girl."

"Whatever."

"Well, Kane, are you working for me or not?"

"All right, but who exactly do I take orders from?"

"Me."

"And what am I to do?"

Finn nodded at his son. "Keep him out of trouble."

"I'll do my best. What's the job?"

"Kyran knows what to do. It's in London. You'll go down there, and once the job is done, you'll come right back."

"If you say so."

"Good."

"When do we leave?"

"Right now."

Kyran glared at his father as he put his coffee cup on the counter. Then he started toward the door. Over his shoulder, he said, "Bring your gun."

"I intend to." Looking at Keira, he smiled and said, "Thanks for breakfast."

———

LONDON, ENGLAND

They pulled up outside a fenced warehouse on the outskirts of London and had to wait several minutes to be let in. A man wearing BDUs appeared, unlocked the gate, and allowed them through.

Once inside, Kyran drove around the side to where a large door opened to admit the vehicle before closing behind them.

Ten men stood waiting as the vehicle slowed to a

stop. Most were dressed like the one who'd let them in. Kyran climbed out, and Kane followed his lead. A man stepped forward and said, "Where's your da? I thought he was coming."

"He sent me instead."

"What the fuck, Kyran?"

"What happened?"

"A couple of assholes blew up the primary warehouse with the lorry in it. Killed a few of our boys, too."

"Who were they?"

The man shrugged. "How should I fucking know? They could be MI5 for all I know."

"What about security?" Kyran asked. "Didn't you have any?"

"Sure, we did."

"Then how did they get in, Mickey? Tell me that."

"I don't know."

"Now we have to get another lorry because you fucked up."

"It weren't my fault," the man protested, his voice whiny.

Kane could see what was about to happen but could do nothing to stop it. A handgun appeared in Kyran's hand, and then it went off. The man called Mickey crumpled to the concrete floor, never to move again.

Kyran looked at the others, his gaze menacing. Then he picked out another man. "Michael, you're in charge. Tonight, you will come with us, and we'll get another lorry."

"Who's he?" Michael asked.

"John. My father employed him."

"Kind of late to bring in new people, isn't it?"

"Are you going to argue with him?"

"Just pointing out that it could lead to problems," the man replied. "How do you know he isn't a plant?"

"Just shut up and do what I ask you to."

"All right, but I'm protesting him having anything —" The man stopped. Kyran's face had taken on a new expression, that of a child about to throw a tantrum. "Listen, just forget about it."

Kyran's expression changed, like a bomb being defused right before it exploded. It was then that Kane learned just how dangerous Finn's son was. He reached into his pocket, and by using touch alone, dialed Cara's cell.

Michael said, "Where do you figure on getting another lorry on short notice?"

"I know a place."

The Irishman nodded. "All right, you're the boss."

"I'm glad you understand it."

———

With no comms, Kane hoped Cara and Knocker were still on the ball, which they were. They were parked a block away from the warehouse in a position conducive to surveillance.

"What do you figure they're doing in there?" Knocker asked.

"Who knows?" Cara replied.

"You want to go and have a look?"

"No. We stay here."

"We need to get eyes on, Cara," the Brit said. "Kane has no comms, so we're flying deaf."

"Don't you mean blind?"

"That too."

Cara's cell phone rang. She looked at the screen and recognized the number, so she answered the call. "Hello, Mollie's Patisserie?"

There was no one on the other end at first. Then she heard the distant voices. Kane was using his cell as a way for them to listen in. She put it on speaker and held her finger to her lips so Knocker would remain silent.

They could only pick up bits of the conversation. Something about a lorry and a voice telling Kane that when they went out later, he would be driving.

"Sounds like they're planning something," Knocker said. "Maybe another lorry?"

"Not surprising, seeing as the others blew up the last one. Keep listening. I'm going to call it in."

She stepped out of the back of the van, careful not to expose herself, and said in a low voice, "Zero, copy?"

"Copy, Reaper Two. Sitrep?"

"Kane has contacted us by cell."

"What did he have to say?"

"Nothing. He called so we could listen in on what was happening. It sounds like they're going after another lorry tonight."

"Makes sense."

"What are your orders?"

"Keep following them. See what happens."

"Do you want us to intercede when they try for the lorry?" Cara asked, almost certain she knew the answer.

"Negative. Let it play out."

"Roger that."

Cara disconnected and climbed back into the van.

"Anything else happen?" she asked Knocker in a low whisper.

"Kane disconnected. Maybe saving his battery."

"Maybe. But did you get anything else?"

He shook his head. "Negative. We'll just have to follow them and see."

CHAPTER 9

LONDON, ENGLAND

THEY LEFT when it was dark. Kyran came up to Kane. "You're driving."

"Where to?"

"I'll give you directions," he replied.

Kane shrugged. "You're the boss."

They left the yard ten minutes later, and Kyran did as he'd said he would. They drove through London for almost an hour. Kane was starting to think Kyran had gotten cold feet since he had him turning left and right and doubling back around the block more than once. It was then that he figured out Kyran was trying to see if he was being followed.

"Are we done fucking around?" Kane asked, trying to keep him focused on the task at hand.

Behind him, Michael said, "If we keep going around in circles, I'm going to throw up in the back here."

"We're being followed."

"Bullshit," Kane said. He was certain Kyran was paranoid since he knew Cara and Knocker were back there somewhere, and he couldn't make them.

"Not bullshit. I'm fucking telling you we're being followed."

"I'm driving, Kyran, and I've been looking in the mirror all the time. There's no one following us. Now, will you tell me where we're going, or do I stop and just get the fuck out?"

"Watch your mouth, American," Kyran growled.

Kane stepped on the brake, and the vehicle stopped suddenly.

"What are you doing?"

"Waiting for you to tell me where we're going."

Kyran's eyes widened, and flecks of spittle passed his lips when he next spoke. His hand went under his coat and brought out the handgun. "Remember who is in charge, Kane, and who holds your life in their hands."

"Hey, calm down, Kyran," Michael said from the back.

"Are we going to do that again?" Kane asked.

"What?"

"The last time you pulled a gun on me, it didn't end that well for you."

The memory returned. A Saab pulled up behind them and blew its horn. Kane said, "Are we going, or what?"

"Fine, drive," Kyran said, putting the handgun away. "Go this way and turn left."

Kane took his foot off the brake, and the vehicle started forward once again.

Thirty minutes later, Kyran ordered him to stop.

Kane figured they were somewhere in the west of London on a suburban street. "Second house on the left. Our target lives there. He owns a trucking company. We'll pick him up and take him to his yard, where we'll steal a lorry. Michael, you come with me. Kane, when you see us come out, drive down and pick us up."

"Does he have any family?" Kane asked.

"So what if he does?"

"I'm coming with you," Kane said, not liking the plan. "Michael can drive."

"You don't give the orders here, Kane. I do."

"Fine. Give the order. I'm going with you."

"Shit, all right."

They climbed out of the vehicle, walked down the sidewalk, keeping to the shadows, and approached the house. When they reached the driveway, Kyran began walking faster. "Wait," Kane hissed.

"What now?"

"It's got a sensor light on the porch. We need to go around the back."

They went past the garage and through the side gate. Kane made sure there was no noise. The last thing he wanted was for someone inside the house to wake up. If that happened, Kyran was likely to lose control, and someone would get hurt.

Once in the back, they walked around to the rear pergola. There was a door that led into a conservatory. Kane tried the knob; it was locked.

Kyran sighed and went to break the glass beside the door. Kane grabbed his arm. "What are you doing? You want to wake everyone up?"

"Do you know another way?"

"Wait here."

Kane walked past the rear of the house, checking the windows until he found one that was unlocked. There always was. He opened it and silently climbed in. He checked for an alarm and figured if there was one, he'd have heard it by now. He went through the kitchen to the conservatory and opened the door. Kyran entered and pushed past Kane.

He made his way through the house, a pen light in his hand. Kane followed him. Suddenly, a Chihuahua came tearing down the hallway. It started barking, and the Team Reaper commander cursed under his breath.

"Shut that fucking thing up," Kyran hissed.

"It's too late for that," Kane pointed out as a light came on farther down the narrow hallway.

"Who's there?" a voice called.

Kane hurried down the hall toward the bedrooms, and as soon as the man appeared, his black hair messed up and his gaze bleary, he placed his weapon against the man's head and said, "No fuss. Just do as we say."

"Harry, what's going on?" a woman asked.

"Tell her to go back to sleep," Kane whispered.

"G-go back to sleep. It's the cat."

"Bloody thing. Turn the light off, will you?"

"You do it. I need to take a piss."

The woman mumbled an expletive and turned off the lamp on the man's side of the bed. Kyran started to walk past the two toward the bedroom. Kane stopped him. "Where are you going?"

"No wit—"

"Fuck off," Kane hissed. "We got what we came for, now move."

"We're not done with this," Kyran said. "I'll tell my father when we get back."

"You know what? For someone who thinks he's smart, you're a dumb fuck with a big mouth."

"What?"

"Just move," Kane whispered and pushed Harry before him.

Kane escorted the man to the kitchen. "You need your work keys."

"Work keys?" Harry asked.

"Yes, where are they?"

"In the fruit bowl."

"Get them."

Harry did as he was ordered. Kane then escorted him out through the conservatory. The man stopped suddenly. "Please don't kill me."

"I'm not going to kill you as long as you do what we say."

"Sure, fine. I'll do whatever you want."

"Good. Keep moving."

Behind them, Kyran followed in a brooding kind of mood. He was still bent out of shape from Kane ordering him around, and the Team Reaper commander figured he was plotting his revenge.

Michael pulled up out front, and Kane put Harry in the back seat and climbed in beside him. They drove away.

———

"You see that?" Knocker asked rhetorically.

"What do you figure they want with him?"

"I guess we could find out," the Brit said. "Bravo

Four, I'm going to give you an address. Can you run it for me?"

Cara pulled away from the curb and followed the vehicle ahead of them.

"Send it, Reaper Three," Swift replied.

Knocker gave him the address, and within moments, they had their information. "The house belongs to Harry and Linda Groves. Harry is the yard manager at a trucking company in Shredding Green."

"That's where they intend to get the lorry from," Cara said, taking a right turn. "If we hang back, can you direct us to the location, Slick?"

"Consider it done."

"Also, they're likely to have security. Can you put Zero on?"

"I'm here, Reaper Two," Ferrero said.

"Luis, can we do something about the security at the company yard?"

"I'll see to it. It is thirty minutes max from where you are to the destination. We'll have the yard evacuated by then so they can get their lorry."

Suddenly the van chugged and then stopped. "Shit," Cara hissed.

"What's up?"

"The van just shit itself for some reason. It's dead—electronics, the works."

Swift came on the comms, a hint of urgency in his voice. "Reaper Two, I'm getting a radio signal in your vicinity. Close by."

"Fuck," Knocker growled and grabbed for his and Cara's M6s. "Some cock disabled the van. They're onto us."

A Land Rover appeared out of the darkness, and four shooters in tactical equipment emerged.

Knocker tossed Cara a weapon as she was climbing into the rear. There was a tumultuous roar, and the van was lit up by automatic gunfire. Bullets punched through the thin metal encompassing it, providing no protection for any within. They barely missing both occupants as they dived to the floor.

Cara felt the burn of a bullet as it ripped through fabric and scored her ribs. "Son of a bitch!" she yelped.

"You alright?" Knocker shouted at her as the interior equipment exploded and rained down on them.

"Just fucking wonderful."

The bullets kept coming, punching holes in the van and leaving it looking like Swiss cheese. Then the gunfire stopped. Knocker said, "Reloading. Let's go."

Fully aware that they wore no body armor, Cara nodded. "On you."

Knocker burst through the rear door of the van, the M6 up and sweeping for targets. He moved quickly around the van, Cara close behind him. The gunfire started again, and they were both happy to have the vehicle between them and the shooters.

"Zero, this is Reaper Two. We are in contact. I say again, we're in contact. Enemy, unknown number."

"Roger, Reaper Two. We're informing the Met. Hang in there."

Cara edged around the end of the van and opened fire at a shooter who was leaning across the hood of a Land Rover. Both bullets ricocheted off the hood. One whizzed past the shooter's ear and the other smashed into the center of his face, making a horrible mess of his once-handsome features.

He reeled back. Cara fired a third shot and the man disappeared, falling backward.

The death of their comrade brought even heavier fire on the team members' position. Knocker looked at her. "Did you have to piss them off?"

"Shut up and shoot."

Knocker moved to the front of the van and began to fire. He blazed through half a magazine, trying to suppress the shooters. As he did so, he figured out there were three more opposite them.

"Those guys aren't fucking Irish," Knocker shouted to Cara.

"What?" she called back, opening fire.

"They're not Irish."

"Why do you say that?"

"Trust me. The IRA splinter cells don't deck their people out like that. They're someone else."

"If we get out of this, we might be able to figure it out."

Knocker sighted on a shooter and squeezed the trigger. The man's head snapped back, and he fell to the ground. "We're one body closer to doing that."

Two down, two to go.

Cara and Knocker needn't have worried about it, however. The shooters disappeared into the darkness as silently as they'd come, leaving behind their transport and their two dead comrades.

The area was silent, but Knocker and Cara waited several minutes before cautiously approaching the two fallen men, worried that their friends would reappear. Once they'd ascertained that they were dead, Knocker took his cell out and took a picture of the shooter who was still recognizable.

"Slick, I'm sending you a picture."

"Copy that. Get fingerprints too."

"How am I meant to do that?"

"I put a new app on your cell before you went out," the tech explained. "It'll allow you to do it."

"Sweet."

He found the app, and took the two fallen shooters' prints, and sent them back. "You will have them about now."

"Great. The police should be there shortly."

Cara said, "I can hear the sirens. Do they know who we are?"

"Yes, they do."

"Thanks. Reaper Two out."

"Cara," Knocker called.

"What?"

"Have a look at this guy."

She walked over to where Knocker stood. "What's up?"

"This guy look Middle Eastern to you?"

"He doesn't look like your typical Irishman."

Knocker nodded. "Tied up with the terrorists who bombed the bridges, do you think?"

"I doubt it. The Met and MI5 rolled them all up."

"That leaves Libya."

"Shit, that's all we need," Cara growled. "Zero, copy?"

"I'm here, Reaper Two."

"These guys appear Middle Eastern. We're thinking they might be Libyan."

"Terrorists?"

"No," said Knocker as he squatted beside one of the dead men.

The sirens were getting even louder.

"What makes you so sure?" Cara asked.

"I just found a tattoo," he explained. "They're Al-Saiqa. Libyan Special Forces."

"Shit."

———

"Are we sure?" Thurston asked Ferrero.

"Slick confirmed it minutes after they informed us on the ground. Both facial and fingerprint."

"I'll have to inform MI5. Of course, they'll head for their embassy."

"I would imagine so."

"It has to be related to the mission in Libya," Thurston said. "Could it be a splinter faction?"

"It's possible but unlikely. If Slick can get access to any cameras near the embassy, we'll know. If they show up, then it was state-sanctioned."

"How did they know it was us. The whole thing was targeted."

"Besides all the bad guys, who doesn't like us at the moment?"

"The director of National Intelligence, Brett Edison."

Ferrero nodded. "That would be my guess."

"Which means he has someone on us," Thurston theorized. "Son of a bitch. He wants to take us off the map because we made him look bad, but he hasn't got the balls to do it himself."

"What would you like me to do?"

"Nothing. I'll take care of it."

"All right."

"Any news from Kane?"

"No, but the last we knew, he was with Kyran Finn, and they were going to get another lorry."

"Is Slick tracking them?"

"No. We know where they're going."

"All right. Keep me updated."

———

The vehicle pulled up outside the trucking yard in front of two large gates. Kyran looked left and right. "Where's the security guard?"

"I-I don't know," Harry replied.

"Get the gate open."

Kane and Harry climbed out, and the manager used his keys to undo the lock on the steel-mesh gates. They swung them open and allowed Michael to drive through, then closed them behind him without locking them. As they did, Kane said, "Just do everything we ask. Don't give him an excuse to kill you. I'll do all I can to keep you safe."

"Who are you?"

"That doesn't matter."

Kyran got out of the vehicle, as did Michael. "Are the keys in the office?"

"Yes," Harry replied.

The younger Finn looked at the lorries and pointed at a small van with a square box on the back that looked like an ice cream truck. "That one."

"I'll have to go into the office to get the keys."

"Kane will go with you."

The Team Reaper commander didn't miss the open use of his name. He said, "Come on, Harry."

The scared man showed Kane to the office. It was a clean and spartan place with an industrial feel.

"The keys are in the safe."

"Get them." Reaper looked around to make sure they were alone.

Harry knelt on the polished linoleum floor and started to turn the knob. After a few spins, he tried to open it. He gasped when it remained closed.

Kane said, "Just relax, Harry. I meant what I said. You get me the keys, and I'll tie you up here for your people to find in the morning. All right?"

"I-I..."

"I know you're scared, but I'm not going to let anything happen to you. Trust me."

The safe opened. Harry reached inside and took out the keys. "These ones," he said, handing them over.

"Get on the chair," Kane said, pointing at an office chair.

Harry sat down.

"You have any duct tape?"

"Tape?"

"Yes, tape. Thick stuff that fixes anything."

"I know what it is."

"Well?"

"In the drawer."

Kane found it and taped Harry to the chair. "I'm going to tape your mouth, Harry. But don't worry, someone will find you in the morning."

"Who are you?" Harry asked again.

"Not who you think," Kane replied and placed a strip of tape over his mouth. "Get some sleep."

Kane left the office and walked outside into the damp night. It was the first time he'd noticed the cold in a while. Kyran looked at him and asked, "Where's the yoke?"

"What?"

"The man who was with you," the younger Finn said.

"He's taped to a chair in the office."

Kyran nodded. "Take the keys and help Michael get it started."

They walked over to the delivery lorry and cranked it. "I'll be seeing you, Kane," Michael said. "Watch your back with Kyran."

"I already am. What do they need the lorry for anyway?"

"They didn't tell you?"

"If I was any further in the dark, I'd be in a black fucking hole."

"Let's just say it'll make people sit up and listen."

"Another bomb?" Kane asked.

"Not this time."

The lorry roared as it drove out of the yard, and Kane was left choking on diesel fumes as he watched it go. He turned to find out what Kyran was up to and couldn't see him. He figured he must have climbed into the vehicle, so he started walking toward it. He reached it and looked inside. No Kyran. Then he heard the gunshot. His heart leaped.

"Oh, fuck, no," he blurted and started running.

Kane met him coming out of the office. Kyran was putting his gun away when he looked up and saw Kane standing there. The Reaper came out to play as rage consumed Kane. He dragged the younger Finn off the office steps, threw him to the ground, and followed him. "You murdering son of a bitch," Kane hissed.

"What the fu—" Kyran's words were rammed back down his throat with one punch from Kane. Blood flew, and Kane hit him again. This time he broke his nose.

Kane started to drag the young Irishman to his feet. "Get the fuck up."

Kyran staggered to his feet and made a grab for his handgun. Kane had known he would and hit him again. He then took the handgun from him and tucked it into his pants.

Once again, the Team Reaper commander hauled him to his feet before dragging him to their ride. After opening the passenger door, he threw Kyran in. "Put your seatbelt on, shithead."

He walked back around and climbed into the driver's seat before starting the motor and driving out of the yard.

"You're dead," Kyran spluttered through the blood.

"Just shut up," Kane growled. "The man was no problem to you. There was no need to shoot him."

"No witnesses."

"Dickhead," Kane snapped and drove faster.

CHAPTER 10

LONDON, ENGLAND

"WE HAVE A PROBLEM," Thurston told Fitzgerald over the phone.

"Don't you ever sleep?" he asked.

"Not when I have ops running," Thurston replied.

"What is the drama?"

"Libyan Special forces tried to kill two of my people tonight."

"Are you sure they were Libyan?"

"Facial recognition, fingerprints, and the two remaining shooters were pictured going into the Libyan Embassy in Ennismore gardens."

"Bugger," Fitzgerald said.

"That's not the worst of it," Thurston continued. "It was a targeted attack in retaliation for our incursion onto their soil. The only way they would know that was if they were told."

"Who would do that?"

"Brett Edison, head of National Intelligence."

"The one responsible for your current predicament?"

"That's the worm. Do you think you could put someone outside where we're operating from? We think we have a watcher."

"I'll get my people on it. We'll fix your problem."

"Thank you. But what are we going to do about the Libyan thing?" Thurston asked.

"We'll let the politicians sort that one out. Do you have anything for me?"

"Kane has infiltrated the Finn organization. Right at this time, they're stealing a lorry for their cause," Thurston informed him.

"Really? You people work fast." There was surprise in Fitzgerald's voice. "What's the plan?"

"See it through and try to figure out what the target is."

"Great. Good luck. Keep me apprised."

"Roger that."

————

NOTTINGHAMSHIRE, ENGLAND

"What the hell happened to you?" Finn asked gruffly, staring at his son's swollen face.

"Your fucking boy there is what happened, Da," Kyran snapped.

Finn might have had issues with his son, but when all was said and done, the younger Finn was his flesh and blood. He glared at Kane. "Go see your sister. Have her look at you."

"Just have Braden shoot him, Da."

"Go, boy."

Kyran left the living room in a huff, much like a spoiled child. Finn said, "Before I do what he suggests, tell me what happened."

"He pissed me off," Kane replied stoically.

"Is that it?"

"No. He shot a guy I had secured to a chair. There was no reason for it. He did it anyway."

"And you beat the shite out of him for that?" Finn snarled.

"Yes, I did."

The Irishman nodded. Kane's weapon appeared in his right hand; in his left was Kyran's handgun. One was pointed at O'Connor, the other at Finn. "Do we really want to do this?" Kane asked.

"You won't need that, Kane," Finn said. "You've proven yourself, which was why I sent you with Kyran. You won't put up with his shite and are prepared to follow through on your convictions. And while I still don't like what you did, you are a man I can use."

"Speaking of that," Kane said, "no one has even told me what it is I'm supposed to be doing."

"All will be revealed later this morning," Finn replied. "For now, get some sleep."

Kane was allowed to go to the room he'd slept in before. He closed the door and listened quietly to see if someone had followed him and was outside in the hall-way. When he was certain there was no one there, he took out his cell and turned it on. He dialed a number, and Thurston came on the line. "About damned time—"

"Ma'am, I don't have much time," Kane said,

cutting her off. "Whatever is happening will go down tomorrow."

"Are you sure?"

"I don't know, but there is a good chance. Also, there is a dead guy in the office at the trucking company. Kyran Finn shot him after I tied him up and left him."

"Shit, Reaper."

"I know. I did all I could to keep him alive."

She sighed. "I'm sure you did. What happened to the lorry?"

"It was taken back to the warehouse," Kane replied.

"What warehouse?"

"I'm not sure. There was a passel of men there as well. They looked military. Maybe former Army."

"Possibly the ones who ran from the other warehouse," Thurston theorized.

There was a soft footfall in the hallway on the other side of the door. Kane lowered his voice. "I have to go. I'll check in when I know more."

"Take care."

"Yes, ma'am."

A soft knock came from the door. Kane walked over to it and found Keira Walsh standing there in a pair of pajama shorts and a loose-fitting top. "Shouldn't you be in bed?" Kane asked.

"I would be if you hadn't punched the shite out of my brother," she said curtly.

"I'm sorry, but he had it coming."

"What, he stopped you from shooting a man, and you beat the bejesus out of him?"

"Is that what he told you?"

"That's right."

Kane nodded in understanding. "All right."

"So, you don't deny it?"

The Team Reaper commander shrugged. "Would you believe me if I did?"

"Not for a moment," Keira replied, but her eyes said differently.

"I guess there's nothing to discuss then, is there?" he said, turning away and taking off his shirt and pullover.

He heard her gasp when she saw the tattoo. He turned back and said, "Are you staying or going?"

"What?" she asked with a frown.

"I'm going to bed. It's been a long night. You can either leave and shut the door on your way out, or you can stay. I don't really care."

Kane turned his back on Keira once more and started to remove his pants. Behind him, he heard the door close. Kane turned to find Keira still in his room. He'd thought she would leave, but she hadn't, and he wasn't sure he could go ahead with it. She opened her top, undoing the buttons one at a time, staring at him in silence. She let it slide to the floor, baring her chest. Keira's breasts were not overly large, but they sat high and looked firm to the touch.

"Keira, I—"

She reached out and touched his lips with her finger. "Don't say anything."

Thoughts of Cara ran through Kane's mind, and even though he wanted to, he knew he shouldn't. "Keira, I can't."

"Shh, you can. Don't worry about Da and Kyran."

"I want to, but I can't. There's someone else."

At first, there was embarrassment on her face.

However, that didn't last long. It quickly turned to rage as she bent to retrieve her top.

"Keira, wait."

She whirled. "Fuck you. I open myself to you and this...this..." Her anger got the better of her, and she couldn't go on.

"I'm sorry, Keira."

She ignored him as she shrugged into her top and walked out the door. Feeling like a dick, Kane went to close it, only for O'Connor to appear in front of him. He smiled mirthlessly and said, "Something else Kyran will want to kill you for."

Kane stared at him for a moment before closing the door in his face.

———

Kane was dragged out of his slumber by a loud crash on his door. "Get the fuck up, lad. There's work to be done."

Kane came awake with a start. He stared at the ornately decorated ceiling and waited for his heart rate to slow. Then the events of the previous night came to him, and he sighed regretfully. He rolled over and sat on the side of the bed. The muscles in his back rippled, causing the Reaper tattoo to take on a life of its own.

After a short while, he dressed and went out into the hallway, then downstairs and into the large dining room. Finn was there with his son and daughter, along with O'Connor. Finn looked up from his food. "You look like shite."

Kane pointed at Kyran. "I look better than him."

The younger Finn looked up and balefully glared at him through partially closed eyes. "Fuck you."

"For Christ's sake," Finn growled. "Not again."

Keira ignored everything that was going on around them and concentrated on her food. "What's so urgent?" Kane asked.

"You've got another job today," the Irishman replied.

"What job?"

"I need you to make a delivery for me. There's a lorry in the barn I need taken to inner London."

Kane thought about it. "Is it a bomb?"

"No, it's not a fucking bomb." Finn chuckled. "Don't worry about what it is. Just make sure it gets delivered. Can you do that?"

"Sure. Who's coming with me?"

"One-man job. I'd send Kyran with you, but you'd end up killing him before you got there."

The younger Finn ignored the jibe. "Besides, like I said, it's a one-person job. You can drive a lorry, can't you?"

Kane nodded.

"Good. You leave in fifteen minutes."

The Team Reaper commander sat down and ate a bowl of cereal, something he hadn't done in years. He had to admit it wasn't too bad. When he was almost done, Finn said, "Braden, take him out to the barn and show him the lorry."

O'Connor came to his feet. As he did, his jacket fell open, and Kane saw the butt of a handgun tucked inside a holster. As he walked out of the dining room, Kane passed Keira. She didn't look at him. He needed to apologize to her again. Make it right. But it would have to wait until he returned.

The weather outside was miserable again. The sky was overcast and the day a drab gray, with a cold wind blowing. O'Connor led Kane to the barn, and they entered through a side door. Inside was the lorry.

The enforcer opened the double front doors, then walked back to where Kane stood. He tossed him the keys. "Get her started while I put the address in the navigation device."

Kane nodded and climbed behind the wheel. He put the key in the ignition and turned. The motor cranked over, and soon the lorry was idling quietly. O'Connor hoisted himself into the passenger seat. Kane looked at him and asked, "Why did we have to get another lorry when he already had this one?"

The Irishman gave him a curt answer. "Because the boss said so."

Kane decided not to push it. Kyran was loose-cannon dangerous, but O'Connor, he was cool and calculating—and that made him even more so. At that point, killing the boss' right-hand man wouldn't be the smartest of moves.

O'Connor said, "You're good to go."

Kane watched him climb back out, and he closed the door. The lorry was automatic, so all he had to do was put it Drive and release the brake.

He gave it some gas, and the lorry crawled out of the barn like a beast from the bowels of the earth. Soon Kane was on a narrow road and following the directions to London.

He was fifteen miles away when he pulled over. He got out and checked the rear doors. He was able to open them, which he did, then climbed inside. Cara and Knocker pulled in behind him. They were driving a V8 Range Rover. They followed him into the rear of the lorry, and they found crates packed inside. "I bet I know what's in them," Knocker said.

They cracked the lid on one and found the AK-74s. Knocker gave a low whistle. "That's a lot of firepower."

"Let's have a look at the others."

They lifted the lid on the others and found ammunition and RPGs. "What do you think they want with them?" Cara asked.

"Whatever it is, we need to find out. I'll deliver them and see if I can get an answer."

"Something isn't right about this, Reaper. All this firepower and only one man escorting it," Knocker said.

"Maybe. Just keep me in sight until we get there. You'll need to report it to Thurston or Ferrero as well."

"We'll take care of it," Cara said. She touched his arm. "Take care."

"Always."

They closed the back of the lorry, and Kane was mobile once more. Cara and Knocker did the same, and the Brit grinned at her.

"What's that look for?" Cara asked.

"You and him are bumping uglies."

"Shut up," Cara growled.

"You are, I can tell."

"What kind of a term is that, anyway?"

Knocker shrugged. "One that works."

"Shut up," she growled again and fell in behind Kane and the lorry.

———

When they came, they seemed to fall from the sky. One moment nothing, the next, the firearms unit from the Metropolitan Police swarmed the road with weapons drawn, blocking his passage.

Kane slammed on the brakes to keep from smashing into a police vehicle, the rear tires locking as he did so. "Son of a bitch."

"Get out of the lorry!" an armed officer shouted at him.

"Keep your hands on the wheel!" shouted another.

Kane was confused. "Which fucking one do you want?" he shouted through the windshield.

Behind him in the Range Rover, Cara jammed on the brakes. Knocker said, "Fuck me, this isn't bloody good."

"What the hell is going on?" Cara asked out loud. "Zero, something is wrong. Reaper has just been stopped by a shitload of armed police."

"Roger, we're seeing it from this end. Mary is working on it."

They sat there and watched as the lorry was surrounded by armed men. They could hear the shouts as the officers barked instructions. Overhead, Cara could see a helicopter circling. "This is bullshit," she growled.

"Something isn't right," Knocker stated.

More armed police arrived. More shouting. Then someone fired a shot, and all hell broke loose.

Inside the cab, the first bullet punched through the windshield, narrowly missing Kane. His first instinct was to shout at them not to shoot. However, they were too nervous, so instead, he went for the floor just as they all opened fire.

Rounds hammered into the lorry's cab. The windshield disintegrated, as did the side windows. Kane was showered with glass and debris, but luckily, nothing hit his flesh. He buried his head under his hands as though the futile gesture would save him should one or more of the bullets find him.

After what seemed like an age, he heard someone shouting to cease fire. Slowly, painfully so, the gunfire petered out, and a stunned silence descended over the scene of destruction.

The quiet hung in the air for a while before someone said, "Check the cab. See if he's dead."

Kane heard boots on the road, then the door opened. He looked up and saw two armed policemen standing in the opening. Both had handguns pointed in his direction. "Howdy," Kane said.

"Get out of the cab!" one of them shouted. "Get out of the fucking cab!"

"All right," Kane said calmly. "But don't shoot me."

"Get the fuck out, terrorist bastard."

"What?"

"Move!"

Kane crawled toward the open door and almost got there before the two, armed response officers grabbed him and dragged him the rest of the way. He hit the hard asphalt on the road and grunted. "Take it easy, will you?"

"He's got a gun," one of the men shouted and took Kane's weapon from his pants. A knee landed in the middle of the Team Reaper commander's back, and pain shot up his spine. Kane yelped, and the kneeler must have got satisfaction from it because he added more weight while he cuffed him.

"What the hell is this?" Kane gasped.

"You men check the back of the lorry," a man called.

"Is someone going to tell me what's going on?" Kane asked.

"Roll him over," a voice said. Kane felt the pressure lift from his back, then hands rolled him roughly onto his back.

Kane looked up and saw a police officer standing over him. "Who are you?" he asked. "What's your name?"

"Fred Flintstone. Who are you?"

An armed officer beside Kane kicked him in the ribs with heavy boots. Kane grunted and winced at the pain. "Smart ass, huh? Well, we'll see how smart you are when the intelligence services get hold of you and bury you in a dark hole somewhere."

"Boss, there's weapons and all kinds of shit in the back of this thing," an officer called from the rear of the lorry.

The officer in charge glared at Kane. "Get him on his feet."

Two armed response officers dragged Kane up and pushed him toward the rear of the lorry. The Team Reaper commander became aware of the helicopters overhead. Then he looked around and saw armed police and cop cars as far as the eye could see.

They pulled him up at the back of the lorry, and the armed response commander climbed into the rear and investigated the open crates. "Not what we were expecting, but it'll do." He grunted and turned to stare at Kane. "Where's the explosives?"

"What explosives?"

One of the officers guarding him whacked him in the lower back. Kane gasped and glared at him. "Do that again, and I'll break your nose."

The man, being smart, did it again. Kane had known it was going to happen and brought his head forward so the hard bone of his forehead caught the officer across the bridge of his nose. The man reeled away, blood running down like a faucet.

The second man kicked Kane's legs from beneath him, and he dropped like a stone. Pain shot through his knees and ankle. "Fuck me," he groaned.

The armed response commander jumped down and said, "What's your name?"

"John Kane."

The officer nodded. "That's better. Now, where's the explosives?"

"What explosives?"

"You were meant to be carrying explosives. We got a tip this morning."

"Someone told you wrong," Kane replied.

"What are all the weapons for?"

"I don't know. I was told to take them somewhere."

"Where?" the commander asked.

"To the address in the satnav. Who are you, anyway?"

"Superintendent Granger of the Specialist Firearms Command," the man replied and waved at one of his men to have a look. Meanwhile, the officer that Kane had headbutted was now on his feet, the bottom half of his face red. He took a lunging step toward Kane, and a growl emanated from deep in his throat. Granger held up his hand. "Jones, go and get cleaned up."

The officer stormed off, and the commander turned his attention back to Kane. "What was supposed to happen with the weapons when you got there?"

"I don't know," Kane said with a shrug.

The officer who'd gone to check on the satnav returned and shook his head. "It's stuffed."

"I'm not surprised after what you people did to the lorry," Kane said.

Granger stared at Kane, then said, "Put him somewhere and have two men watch over him. We'll come back to him later."

CHAPTER 11

OUTSIDE LONDON, ENGLAND

KNOCKER AND CARA remained where they were until they were told to move on by a police officer. He came up to their Range Rover, and Cara rolled down the window. "What's going on? Can we get through?"

The officer eyed them suspiciously before shaking his head. "No. You'll have to go around."

"What's happened?" Knocker asked. "What's with all the Bobbies?"

"Nothing to worry about. Just a police operation."

"Is that why you shot the shit out of that lorry?"

"Just turn around, sir, and keep moving."

He walked away, and Cara said, "Someone tipped them off about the lorry. But why?"

"There's only one reason I can think of," Knocker replied. "To take the focus off something else."

"Yes, but what?"

As they continued to watch what was happening ahead of them, Knocker noticed the man in the suit who walked up to the police tape, flashed his identity, and was allowed to pass. The Brit said, "Looks like the intelligence services have arrived. Isn't that Bancroft?"

"Looks like it. Let's hope he can fix this."

———

Kane looked up and saw Bancroft walking toward where he was seated with his two police guards. The MI6 man looked at the closest of the policemen. "I need to talk to your commander."

"Who are you?"

"I'll explain it to him when I see him. Be a good chap and find him for me."

"You a spook?"

Bancroft gave him a mirthless grin, then relaxed his facial muscles. The officer shrugged and said, "I'll be right back."

The MI6 officer looked down at Kane. "Got yourself in a bit of a fix, old boy."

"I've had better days. Right now, I'm trying to figure out why I was set up like this."

"Pissed anyone off lately?"

"Easier to ask who I haven't," Kane replied with a wry smile.

Granger appeared and stared at Bancroft. "Who are you?"

"Bancroft, Special Intelligence Services."

"What can I do for you?"

Bancroft indicated Kane. "I'd like for you to uncuff my friend here."

Granger frowned. "Why?"

"He's working for the British government on something."

"Then what was he doing with a lorry-load of weapons? We got a call saying the lorry was a massive truck bomb."

"You're going to have to trust me when I tell you he's not responsible for this."

"I've just got to take your word for this?"

Bancroft shook his head. "No. I can give you a number to call if that will satisfy you."

Granger stared at him for a moment before saying, "Uncuff him."

"Sir—"

"Just do it."

"Yes, sir."

Kane was uncuffed, and he got to his feet. He smiled at Bancroft. "Thanks."

They walked and talked. "Thurston?"

"Yes, she called me. I happened to be in the area. You want to fill me in?"

"Brian Finn."

"The IRA man?"

"That's him. We've been working him about the bombing at the Exchange. He's good for it, and I managed to get inside."

"You only get inside if he wants you inside," Bancroft said.

"We set up an op with his daughter. It worked out, and everything was fine until I met his son."

"That little fucker is dangerous," Bancroft growled.

"Isn't he just? I don't think much of O'Connor either."

Bancroft nodded. "He's a former British

Commando. Got out after a while and went home to Ireland, where he met up with Finn. Been working for him ever since. Makes problems go away."

"I figured that."

They went under the tape and walked along the road. Kane pointed at the Range Rover. "That's my ride."

Cara and Knocker climbed out and met them in front of the vehicle. Cara asked, "Are you alright?"

"Yes. Barely."

"That was intense, Mucker," Knocker said.

"You should have been in the cab with me."

"Are you thinking what we are?" Cara asked him.

"I don't know. What are you thinking?"

"Finn set you up to take the heat off something else."

Kane nodded. "I thought about that."

Knocker looked at Bancroft. "What's happening in London today?"

"Nothing much."

"Are you sure? Anything important?"

The MI6 man shook his head. "Nothing until tomorrow. The Irish delegation meets with some parliament ministers then."

"Not today?" Kane asked.

"No."

Cara looked thoughtful. "Where are they staying?"

"At an estate in Bedfordshire."

"Out in the country?"

"Yes."

She looked at Kane. He nodded. "Get the team together. It's time to go to work."

"You really think they'll go after them at the estate?"

"I do. Can you get blueprints for the place?"

"Sure, but this is an operation for the SAS."

Kane said, "Reach out to Fitzgerald at MI5. Talk to him."

Bancroft reached into his pocket and took out his cell. After a couple of minutes, he hung up. "He's given you the green light. It's your op."

"I'm not sure if I really want it," Kane replied grimly.

———

FAIRFIELD ESTATE, BEDFORDSHIRE

The delivery lorry pulled up at the main gate to the estate, and the armed security guard walked up to the passenger's window. Kyran rolled down the window, his Beretta below the opening and out of sight. The guard's partner was still in the small shelter where the electronic security system was housed. There was another inside the large three-floor mansion.

The guard at the window asked, "What are you doing here?"

"We've got a delivery to make," Kyran replied.

"It's not on the list."

"What list?"

"The one I checked as you were driving up."

"Shit," Kyran growled. "We've come all the way out here for nothing. Christ, we were told to get it out here today."

"What is it?"

"Meat, vegetables. The boss said the guests were eating like horses and they wanted more food for the kitchen."

The guard gave him a helpless look. "Sorry. If it's not on the list, you don't get past the gate."

Kyran nodded, then brought up his gun and shot him.

The security guard's head snapped back as the hollow point round punched into his skull. The younger Finn came out of the lorry and hurried toward the open pedestrian gate. The other guard stuck his head out of the security hut and received a bullet for his trouble.

He collapsed half in, half out, unmoving.

Kyran went inside, found what he was looking for, and raised the gate. He climbed into the lorry as it drove through the gate.

The driver followed the driveway around to the rear of the mansion. Once there, he stopped and cut the engine. The rear door opened, and eight men climbed out, all armed with AK-74s and wearing tactical gear.

They entered the rear of the building, and within moments, gunshots rang out. The operation was well underway.

———

LONDON, ENGLAND

"We need to get your team airborne, Reaper," Thurston said as the team double-checked their equipment. "Finn's people just took the estate where the Irish delegation is staying. We dropped the fucking ball on this one."

Kane nodded as he finished putting his spare magazines into his pouches. Beside him, Cara tucked the last of her equipment into her duffel. "No, they were always ahead of us. What are the reports saying, General?"

"Multiple casualties and thirty hostages. That's all they've told us."

"You mean we're in contact with them?"

"MI5 is. The terrorists reached out as soon as they took it."

"No demands?" Kane asked.

"No."

"Then why reach out?"

"Because they want publicity. At the same time, they called it in to every tabloid and news station in the country. Have you had a good look at the blueprints?"

Cara nodded. "Yes, ma'am. We figure the best way in is an old smugglers' tunnel under the estate. But..."

"But what?"

Cara glanced sideways at Kane.

"Come on, spit it out. We don't have time."

"I'm going in alone. Try to link up with them and get back on the inside."

"Too dangerous. Absolutely not. You all go in, or no one does. You retake that estate with extreme prejudice. Then everyone gets to go home."

Axe stared at Thurston. "I like that idea better."

"Me too," agreed Knocker. "Fuck the bastards."

"What about Finn?" Cara asked.

"The estate was raided earlier when the call came in. He wasn't there. They picked his daughter up, and she's in MI5 custody being questioned."

"She doesn't know anything," Kane told them.

"What makes you so sure?"

"Trust me, ma'am. She's not one of them."

"All right, I'll have a word with Fitzgerald. Meanwhile, get your asses in the helo."

———

The team had just left when a call came into Thurston. She recognized the voice on the other end immediately: Hank Jones. "Mary, we have a problem."

"That makes two of us, Hank. Tell me about it."

"Alex Joseph just reached out to me from the CIA. It appears our mutual friend in intelligence has just shown his hand."

"Do I want to know?"

"He's just taken Melanie Kane into custody. Word is she's going to be charged with conspiracy against the government."

"You are fucking shitting me," Thurston hissed. "She's been in a coma for years, and they do something like this? There's no way she's well enough to withstand it."

"Nothing we can do about it, I'm afraid."

"When Reaper finds out, there will be," she replied with certainty.

"Tell him nothing, Mary. Not until this op is wrapped up."

"Damn it, Hank!"

"Sorry, Mary, but I'm making it an order. I know you'll follow it."

Thurston screwed her eyes shut. She knew he was

right. "All right, Hank, but as soon as this op is done, I'm telling him."

"No qualms there."

The call disconnected, and she went to find Ferrero. She told him about Melanie and what the general had said. "He's right. If they're not totally focused, people will get killed."

"I still don't like it."

"It is what it is."

She nodded. "Has Slick got a feed into the estate?"

"Just established one, although I don't know for how long. We've also got a bird in the air."

"How?" Thurston asked, surprise in her voice.

"MI5. Gotta love the Security Service."

"Ma'am, do you have a moment?" Swift called from his terminal.

She and Ferrero walked over. "What is it?"

"I just intercepted transmissions coming from and going into the estate."

"Finn?"

"I'm not sure. No names were mentioned."

"What did they say?" Ferrero asked.

"That's just it. Nothing much. It must have been code, but it's not one I know about. They talked about streets in Belfast."

"Get onto it, Slick. See what they were discussing. I want to know."

"Yes, ma'am."

Thurston's encrypted cell rang. She took it out and answered, "Thurston."

"Mary, Frank Fitzgerald. I know you're in the middle of an op, but I have something that might interest you."

"I'm listening."

"Your two Libyan Special Forces guys are about to leave the embassy, on their way to a private airstrip on the outskirts of London."

"Okay."

"The interesting part was that with them will be Abdul Ben Halim, the Libyan head of intelligence. If anyone knows what is going on with the attempt on your people, it's him."

"There's only one way to do that, you realize," Thurston replied.

"I'm aware of that."

"Are you green-lighting us to kidnap a foreign intelligence officer who is possibly traveling under a diplomatic passport?"

"No. That would be illegal. I'm just suggesting that if you need answers, now would be the time to get them."

Thurston thought about it for a moment. "What do we do with him after we're done?"

"I might be able to find somewhere for him. A foreign intelligence official on British soil can cause quite a stir."

"I'll let you know what I decide. How long do I have?"

"An hour, hour and a half at most. Check your secure inbox."

Was there such a thing? "Roger that."

The call disconnected, and she looked at Ferrero. "I need you, Arenas, Traynor, Troy, and Slick *now*."

Five minutes later, they were tucked away from the rest of the team. The grim expression on her face told them their day was going to go downhill on a seriously steep gradient. "What I'm about to ask you to do is illegal and could wind us all up in prison for a long time. At worst, we could finish as prisoners of a foreign government. Anyone who doesn't want to be part of it should leave now."

They glanced at each other, but no one left.

Thurston sighed. "I really wish Knocker were here for this. It would make it a whole lot easier."

"Just tell us, Mary," Ferrero said. "We're all adults."

"I was just talking to Fitzgerald. He informed me that the Libyan Special Forces shooters who attacked our people are about to leave the embassy, along with their head of intelligence, Abdul Ben Halim. MI5 believes he will have all the answers to any questions we may have."

"Are you asking us to go after him, Mary?" Ferrero asked.

"Yes."

They looked at each other. Arenas said, "This is a big ask."

"Yes, it is."

"It could cause a diplomatic incident of epic proportions," Troy pointed out.

"Yes, it could."

"Tell them, Mary," Ferrero said.

"Luis—"

"Do it."

She sighed. "Edison has taken Kane's sister into custody. We believe he was responsible for the Libyans finding out it was us who were in their country. If we can get Halim, it could give us what we need to hold over Edison."

"Say no more," Arenas said, "I will go."

"We'll all go," Troy said. "I know Mel from long ago. If getting this guy means getting her back, then it's a no-brainer."

"All right, gear up. I'll have Slick send you everything you need. Get out of here."

————

Chester Airfield was on the outskirts of London's north side. It had two runways and was mainly used by private commuters. However, being privately owned by Jimmy Kemper, one of many London crime bosses, it was also used by less savory types and had become a backdoor in and out of the country.

This was how the Libyans had managed to get into the country. Now the private government jet waited patiently for its passengers to arrive. Standing outside in a small perimeter were four armed men from the Libyan Special Forces.

"That's their ride," Troy said.

Arenas said into his comms, "Bravo Four, ETA on target?"

"Ten mikes, Zero-Two."

"Good copy. Ten mikes."

He turned to the others. "Any ideas?"

"How about we just walk up to them and take them down?" Troy proposed.

"Good one, Einstein," Traynor replied. "Great way to get killed."

"Got a better idea?"

"No."

"I do," Arenas said. "Are you any good at driving, *amigo*?"

"I can make it go forward."

"That's all we need."

———

The appearance of the black Range Rover put the four men on edge. However, Arenas' plan called for some fancy driving, which he hoped would put them off-guard.

Instead of driving toward them, he used the damp concrete apron as a skid pan, doing handbrake turns, burnouts, and other defensive-driving maneuvers. Then he started to drive circles around the Bombardier Global 5000. What happened next took the guards by surprise.

The front passenger window slid down, and a suppressor attached to an M6A2 carbine appeared. While Troy drove, all of Arenas' marksmanship skills came back to him, and he dropped them one at a time before they could react.

Troy stood on the brakes, and the Rover stopped. Arenas came out of the vehicle smoothly and hurried toward the stairs leading into the plane. Behind him, Troy and Traynor checked the fallen men.

Arenas climbed the steps and stopped in the door-way, letting the M6 hang by its strap as he drew his Glock. He entered the cabin, sweeping left and right. Seeing that it was clear, he moved toward the cockpit. The two pilots turned and saw Arenas standing there wearing a ski mask, his weapon pointed at them. "What are you doing?" one of them blurted. "This is a diplo-matic flight."

"Get up and walk to the rear of the plane," he ordered.

They came out of the cockpit with their hands in the air, passing the intruder before moving to the rear of the cabin.

"Stop there. Face the rear."

They did as they were ordered, and Arenas zip-tied their hands together before gagging them.

"Zero, plane is secure."

"Copy that, Zero-Two. Target is two minutes out."

"Roger that." He paused, then said, "Troy, Pete, two minutes."

They acknowledged his transmission, and they all waited.

———

The black Mercedes pulled up at the base of the steps, then all four doors opened, and a man climbed out of each. There was a flurry of voices, then Arenas heard the first footfall on the bottom step, followed by more. He waited for a moment before stepping forward and filling the doorway. He raised the M6 and centered it on the first man he saw. From the pictures they'd all memorized, Arenas knew this wasn't the man they'd come for.

He stroked the trigger, and the man folded under the strikes of the twin rounds. The sights fell on the next man at the base of the stairs, and he saw it was Halim. He moved his aim to the next man and shot him where he stood.

The last one died with two rounds in him from Troy and Traynor, who'd appeared from behind.

They closed on Halim, who stood there calmly, his jaw firm. "Get on your knees," Arenas snapped.

Halim didn't move.

"Get on your knees *now*."

Halim moved this time. He lowered himself to his knees and finally spoke. "I am a Libyan diplomat. You need to stop what you're doing immediately."

"Tie his hands," Arenas growled, ignoring him.

Troy zip-tied his hands and dragged him to his feet. Then they shoved the intelligence boss toward the area where they had hidden the Range Rover.

Minutes later, leaving the second group of bodies where they lay, they drove away, their package secure.

CHAPTER 12

FAIRFIELD ESTATE, BEDFORDSHIRE

THE TEAM SAT in the trailer of the command lorry, listening to the briefing of the MI5 officer. He was giving them a full rundown of the events so far. Ten armed men inside. Five dead and thirty or so hostages. Eight of them were ministers from Ireland, both sides of the border.

"They are telling us the place is wired with explosives," the officer named Smythe told them. "We have no way of confirming that, so we have to take them at their word."

"Better that way," Kane remarked.

"Much."

"Is the underground tunnel clear?" Cara asked.

"We're not sure."

Kane looked at her. "Take someone with you when we're done here and check."

She nodded. "Knocker."

"Be my pleasure," the Brit replied.

"Has anyone tried to make contact with them since the initial call?" Kane asked.

"Yes, but they haven't answered."

Kane took out his cell. "Give me a minute."

He pressed a few keys and waited. Then, "Who the fuck is this?"

"Hey, Kyran, remember me? I'm the poor fucker you set up with a shipment of weapons."

"No hard feelings. We just needed a distraction."

"Well, it didn't work. I managed to give them the slip."

"Obviously. But in fact, it did work. You see, it had the bastards looking the other way so we could execute our plan."

"Yeah, well, you fucked up there, too."

"What do you mean?"

"How are you going to get out?"

"Why should I tell you?"

"No reason. Where's your father? Is he still at the estate?"

"What's with the questions?" Kyran asked suspiciously. "You working with the police? They offer you some deal?"

"No, I told you, I got away."

"Like fuck you did. You're working for them. Bastard."

The line went dead. Kane shrugged. "It was worth a try."

Smythe said, "No one knows where Finn is, but his son is confirmed to be inside."

"I don't get it. Why would the son do this so openly?"

"We don't know."

"How much time elapsed between them taking this place and word getting out?"

"Not long."

"What was the response time?" Cara asked.

"Thirty minutes."

Cara looked at Kane. "He's not even there. The only ones inside that estate are sacrificial lambs for their cause."

Kane looked at her as though she was crazy. "Keep talking."

"There was a thirty-minute window for him to get out. Hell, they could have taken the estate three times in that amount of time. Then they contacted the proper authorities. Also, Kyran is Finn's son. He's not going to sacrifice him in there like that."

"Then where is he?" Smythe asked.

"Who knows?" Cara said with a shrug. "I'd be more concerned with what they're going to do with this place."

"We need to check that tunnel out," Kane said. "I have a feeling if we don't do something soon, they're going to beat us to it."

————

The tunnel entrance was outside the fence to the east, some two hundred yards away. It was overgrown and smelled wet. Cara and Knocker went inside, hunched over and carrying only their Glocks. Both wore NVGs but carried a flashlight in a pouch.

Knocker hesitated. "I remember a time not so long ago... Something about a tunnel with a snake in it, and the bastard bit me."

"Well, the odds are with you this time," Cara replied.

"How do you figure that?"

"For starters, that one in Libya was in a culvert. This is a tunnel. And the one in the culvert was a cobra. England, and you should know this, has only one venomous snake. The adder."

"I like that."

"Then there are spiders," she said, smiling to herself.

"Fucking cock."

She pushed past him, crouching. The darkness consumed them as they traveled beyond the daylight. "Reaper One, copy? Over."

No answer came to Cara's query. She said, "I guess comms are screwed down here."

"It's the damp," Knocker told her.

"Really?"

"No frigging idea. I just thought it sounded good."

She imagined his shit-eating grin and shook her head. "How are your feet?"

"You wouldn't know they were even there," he replied.

"Are they?"

"Are they what?"

"Still there?"

"Don't know."

"I had to ask," Cara muttered.

She'd gone another twenty yards when she urgently said, "Hold up."

"What is it?" Knocker asked as he froze.

"I've got a tripwire."

"Well, there goes that theory," Knocker said.

"It's hooked up to enough explosives to leave a decent-sized crater in their manicured lawn," Cara said. "Just don't get tangled up in it."

They moved fifty more yards down the tunnel. "Shit."

"What now?"

"Motion sensors."

"Double shit."

"Just back up."

"Did you trigger them?"

"I don't think so, but it rules out going this way."

Knocker nodded. "All right—"

His voice was drowned out by a loud roar. His eyes widened behind the NVGs he wore, and his mouth opened. He threw himself at Cara, forcing her to the damp floor of the tunnel. Knocker closed his eyes and felt the warmth of the explosion wash over them. Then everything went black.

———

Brick looked at Kane, his concern unmistakable. "Was that what I think it was?"

The door of the command trailer was flung open. A policeman stood there, the urgency on his face evident for all to see. "There's been an explosion in the smugglers' tunnel."

"Shit," Kane growled and bounded for the door.

Brick and Axe were hot on his heels. They ran hard for the tunnel mouth, but by the time they reached it, the smoke from the blast was flowing from three places: the tunnel mouth and two craters on the other side of the estate fence.

Kane started to go into the tunnel, but Brick grabbed him. "Hold up, Reaper. You can't go in there. You don't have the equipment."

Kane whirled and looked at the others who had gathered. "Who's got a flashlight?"

An officer stepped forward and reached into his pocket. "It's not much—"

Kane snatched it out of his grasp and started into the still-smoking passageway. He made it all of ten yards before he was forced back, his chest heaving with wracking coughs. He sat down on the ground and put his head between his knees, then let out an angry howl of rage because he'd just lost two integral members of his team—one of whom he suddenly realized he loved.

———

"You still alive?" Knocker asked between coughs.

"I shouldn't be," Cara replied. "Not after what you just did to me."

"Can you see anything?"

"Not much."

"I guess the motion sensors were tripped."

"No shit," Cara growled.

"There's only one thing for it. We keep going."

"They—" She coughed several times. "They'll be expecting us."

"Maybe they'll think we're dead."

"Let's find out."

They pushed on. The dust inside the tunnel made it hard to see. That, combined with the smoke and everything else from the blast, made for tough going, but eventually, they reached their destination: a wooden door, closed but not locked.

Cara went through first. The door opened into a cellar. Once inside, she went to try her comms, but Knocker grabbed her arm and pointed at the far corner of the room. On a stack of crates was a bundle of wires running to plastic explosive bricks bound together by tape, with some type of electronic trigger device attached.

"Might go boom, ma'am," he said quietly.

"What are the odds?" she asked skeptically.

"Probably one percent, but I'd hate to be hanged by them."

She nodded. "All right, what do you propose?"

"We go loud?"

"And they start to kill everyone."

"But it might have the effect of bringing the rest of the team running."

"How about we find somewhere quiet where we can make contact with the others?"

"That might work," Knocker allowed.

They reached into the pouches on their webbing and took out suppressors. Screwing them on, the pair started silently toward the stairs.

At the top, they found another door. This one was unlocked too. Cara opened it a crack and peered through. The hallway beyond was empty. She closed it and said, "We go up. We're not going to get out of here in a hurry. They'll have cleared the floors and have all the prisoners downstairs, so it makes sense."

"No argument from this sod."

She opened the door once more to make sure it was still clear, then walked into the hall. She swept left and right before moving left. "Bravo Four, kill the camera feed."

"Say again. Who is this?"

"Kill the fucking cameras, Slick, before they see us," Cara whispered harshly.

"Holy shit, you're alive."

"Just do it, you bloody scouser," Knocker growled.

A few heartbeats later, he came back. "Cameras are down."

"Good. Now let Reaper know we're still in the land of the living."

"On it."

Cara and Knocker stayed in motion. They were halfway down the hall when a terrorist materialized in front of them. It was just dumb luck that he looked the other way first, which gave Cara and Knocker time to step into an alcove. The masked person turned and went back the way he'd come.

The two intruders came out of the alcove and started down the hallway once more. Pausing at the passage where the terrorist had gone, they saw that he was still facing the other way, so they slid past stealthily and kept walking.

When they reached a set of stairs with dark-wood balustrades, they ascended, sweeping their Glocks before and behind as they climbed, their heads constantly swiveling.

"Where are you?" Swift asked.

"We've just reached the top of some stairs on the second floor."

"Is the hallway clear?"

"Do you hear us shooting?" Cara asked.

"Sorry, habit. From what we know, the rooms

should be all clear. If you lay up in one of them, it'll give you time to regroup."

"Roger that."

Knocker touched Cara's shoulder and pointed at a well-placed block of explosives above their heads. "I guess we know now."

"Shit."

They hurried across the hall and tried one of the doors, but it was locked. Knocker eased Cara aside. "Allow me, my lady."

"Don't you kick the shit out of that."

"Wouldn't dream of it."

Knocker grasped the handle, took a deep breath, and grunted. Cara didn't see what he did, but the door opened. They hurried inside and closed the door after them.

Out of habit, they cleared the room before settling down. Then Cara said into her comms, "Reaper, copy?"

"Read you Lima Charlie, Reaper Two," Kane replied. "It's good to hear your voice."

The relief was evident in his voice.

"You too, Reaper. Listen, we're holed up in a room on the second floor. We've come across two packs of explosives so far. There's bound to be more."

"We can't breach while they're in place. You're going to have to locate each block and take them out."

"I was afraid you'd say that."

Knocker looked at her and winked. "I've got this. Disarming things that go bang is my forte."

"That's a big word."

"Just like my—"

"I don't need to know."

"Brain."

"All right, Reaper, we'll give it a try. Just be ready to come running when we give you the word."

"We'll be here."

Kane signed off, and Cara looked at Knocker. "Let's do this."

———

The noise sounded like a dry twig snapping. The terrorist's neck separated under the force the Brit used on it. The man went limp, and Knocker lowered him to the floor. So far, he'd managed to disarm four devices without having to kill anyone. Those four had taken thirty minutes.

"Ma'am," Knocker said, "there's no guarantee that we're going to get all of these devices. There's only one way we can make sure of them all."

Cara knew where he was going. They had to secure the trigger, and to do that, they would have to find the man who was in control of it. "Do you have a plan?"

"Maybe."

"Do I want to know what it is?"

"Most likely not."

"I didn't think so."

———

Knocker was now armed with an AK-74 he'd taken from the terrorist he'd killed. He also wore his ski mask. His Glock was tucked into the back waistband of his pants. He still wore his body armor because it was almost the same as that of the man he'd killed.

Cara walked in front of him, her hands behind her

back, secured with a zip-tie he'd found on the dead terrorist. They'd nicked the tie, so any force applied would snap the plastic, and Cara's hands would be free. Her Glock was also tucked in her pants, within easy reach.

They'd not gone far when they found another guard. He turned and looked at them. "What the fuck have you got there?"

Cara almost groaned, but the accent Knocker produced was quite convincing. "The bitch was hiding in one of the rooms."

The terrorist stared at her. He walked closer and ran his gaze up and down Cara, then stared at her face. Gone were the dirt and grime she'd brought with her from the tunnel. The dark smudges on her clothes, on the other hand, couldn't be helped. When his gaze lingered on them for too long, Knocker said, "She's a nice piece of ass, huh?"

The man snapped his gaze back to Knocker. "Aye. Be a good root if we had the time."

"We could always make time," Knocker replied.

"What? Michael will go off his fucking nut."

"Only if he finds out. Where is he?"

"In the ballroom with the hostages."

"Then he won't know, will he?"

Cara took a step back, but Knocker shoved her forward. "What do you say? You want a piece?"

The terrorist licked his lips. The Brit could tell he was torn. Knocker reached around and grabbed a handful of Cara's left breast. He squeezed it firmly but not too hard. She shrugged off the hand and said, "Ow, what the fuck? Don't, please."

Suddenly the man nodded. "All right, there's a

room over there." He pointed at a door across the hall, and they walked toward it. Knocker kept his arm around Cara, forcing her forward, and Cara played her part and tried to resist. The terrorist opened the door, and they went in.

"Shut the door," Knocker said.

The man did, and once it was locked, he turned and walked into the butt of the AK-74. He dropped like a stone and didn't move.

Cara looked at him. "Did you have a good feel?"

"Had to make it look real," he said. There was no joy in his voice, just a businesslike tone. "Come on. Let's go."

Once they were back out into the hallway, they kept moving until they came to the foyer. In the spacious entrance, two more terrorists stood guard, both armed with AKs. At the movement of the team members, the pair turned and looked to see who was walking across the white marble-tiled floor. Knocker, while paying attention to them, was also looking at the large explosive charges above the entry.

Cara had seen them too.

The two terrorists watched them approach the open double doors leading to the ballroom. They didn't, however, say a thing.

Inside the ballroom, the hostages were sitting in a tight group on the polished floor in the center of the room. Off to one side were two bodies. Both lay in pools of blood.

Knocker and Cara did a quick scan of the room to evaluate the situation. Six shooters were scattered around the perimeter. One of them, a man who was talking on a cell phone, looked up and said, "What the hell are you doing in here? Get back—" He looked at Cara. "Where did the bitch come from?"

"I found her wandering upstairs."

"What the fuck were you doing upstairs? Everyone was told to remain down here."

Cara's arms moved slightly, and a glance showed that the zip-tie was broken. Knocker kept as close to her as he could so she could get to her handgun without being seen. Her hand wrapped around it and the muscles in her shoulder bunched, ready to unleash their power.

"Wait," Knocker whispered.

"Well?" Michael asked.

Knocker shrugged.

The terrorist's hands moved, and in his left, Knocker saw the trigger. "I have eyes on the trigger."

Outside, the sound of an explosion rattled the windows. All eyes except the Brit's and Cara's looked toward the source of the noise.

"Now," Knocker said.

The two suppressed Glocks came free, and they went to work. Cara's first shot hit Michael in the head. The bullet made mush of his brain before it exited and sprayed blood and gray matter across the room. There was not a twitch, and the trigger fell from his grasp and onto the floor.

Behind her, Knocker was also moving fast. After shooting the first man he saw in the chest, he switched to the second, hitting him in the same place. He shot them both in the head as they tried to come to terms with being shot in the body armor.

Meanwhile, Cara had put her second shooter down. This one got it in the face.

That left two in the ballroom. By then, the crowd had realized that something was awfully wrong, and they were beginning to panic.

The two team members took one terrorist each and dispatched them with ease. That left the ones they'd passed in the foyer earlier.

The terrorists burst through the doors and ran into a hailstorm of lead. They lived long enough for shock to register on their faces before their hearts stopped beating.

"By my calculations, that's about it," Knocker said.

"Let's hope so." Cara turned to the hostages, most of whom were whimpering in fear. "All right, everyone. Just remain calm and stay where you are. Knocker, the explosives at the front entrance."

"Yes, ma'am."

She walked over to where Michael lay and bent down to pick up the detonator. As she did, she said, "Reaper One, we have control of the situation in here. Send in the cavalry."

"Roger that."

In London, another bomb went off.

CHAPTER 13

LONDON, ENGLAND

"WHAT ARE WE LOOKING AT?" Thurston asked as she stared at the big screen.

"What's left of the Mountbatten Arms," Swift said. "It was a hotel built not long after Mountbatten was killed back in the day. It was named in his honor."

"No guesses about who was behind this," Thurston said grimly. "What's the toll so far?"

"Nothing confirmed yet, but it's estimated to be in the hundreds."

Air hissed between her lips. "Shit."

"Do we have any feed?" she asked, her face a mask of concern.

"I've managed to find some."

"Keep sifting through everything you can find."

"Yes, ma'am."

"And—" She stopped as the team walked into the makeshift ops room. "Just do what you can, Slick."

Kane and Cara came over to her. "How bad is it?" he asked.

"Pretty bad."

"What is there for us to do?"

"Nothing at the moment," she said, then added, "but I do need to talk to you about something. Come with me." She looked at Cara. "You, too."

She led them to a quiet room and had them sit down.

Kane frowned. "It has to be something bad."

"It's not good news that I have to share," Thurston allowed. "Edison found out Melanie was awake and took her into custody."

"He what?" Kane exploded out of his chair, stalking across the room to look out a window.

"Easy, Reaper," Thurston said in a low voice, turning to face him. "We know what this is about."

"It's about all of us, isn't it?" He made a fist and punched into the open palm of his other hand.

"That's right."

"He's trying to lure us back to the States so he can sweep us up."

The former general nodded. "That's why we have to think this through before we react."

"Shit, General, she's just out of a fucking coma." Kane rubbed both hands through his hair in frustration.

"I know, Reaper."

Cara walked over to him and touched his arm. "We'll think of something."

"I know how to fix it," Kane growled.

"Alex Joseph is keeping an eye on things for us," Thurston said. "He won't let this get out of hand."

"Do we know where they are holding her?"

"A facility outside DC."

Kane nodded.

Thurston said, "Right now, we need to concentrate on the latest bombing. I'm expecting Fitzgerald here for a briefing any time now. He'll want a full rundown of what happened at the estate."

"They were going to blow it," Kane said. "Pure and simple. Any idea where Finn is?"

"None. But while you're waiting, there is someone you might want to talk to."

———

Knocker entered the room and stopped just inside the doorway. On the other side of the two-way mirror, Ferrero said, "Are you sure about this?"

"Oh, yeah. If there's anyone who can get what we need, it's Knocker."

On the other side, Abdul Ben Halim looked at the former SAS man but remained silent. Knocker did the same: just stood there, his arms folded. The Brit knew the intelligence man would see through any of the shit he tried, so why not try something else? Knocker took a few steps forward and said, "You've got some fucking big snakes in your country."

Halim just stared at him. Knocker pulled the neck of his shirt to expose the flesh. "Fucker got me right there."

The Libyan looked puzzled. "You are still alive."

"Yeah. Dry bite, apparently. Lucky as hell. The terrorist guy who was with us, he got bit too. Ruined his day."

"You were with them." Statement.

"Yeah, I was. The cock we were after was behind the bombings in London."

"How do you know this?"

"How did you know it was us? Who told you?"

"I ask you first, Englishman."

Knocker stared at him. Then he nodded. "All right. I tell you what. I answer, you answer. Cool?"

Halim grunted.

"Right. Our intelligence linked the bombers to Hasan Kubar. Your turn."

"A mutual friend told us it was you."

Knocker nodded slowly.

Halim spoke again. "They were British SAS, those who came first?"

"Yes. Who was the mutual friend?"

"He is American. Were they after Kubar?"

"Yes. What American?"

"I'm not sure of his name."

"Not good enough. We're being straight, remember? Try again."

"I think he works for National Intelligence."

"Edison?"

"Yes."

Knocker held back the smile.

"What did he offer you?" Knocker asked.

"You first. What were the soldiers' names?"

The Brit shook his head. "Not going to happen. They are being dealt with by the government."

"Then our deal ends here."

Knocker stared at him and could tell by the set of his jaw that he wasn't going to get any further. "Don't go anywhere."

Knocker left the room.

"What do you think?"

"You can't give him the names of Regiment operators," Fitzgerald stated.

"What can we give him?" Kane asked.

"Nothing."

"What about his freedom?" Knocker said. "We can give him that."

Fitzgerald shook his head again. "No. He's a foreign intelligence operative conducting an operation—"

"Bollocks."

The MI5 head stopped. "What?"

"Didn't understand? I'll make it clearer."

"Knocker," Thurston cautioned.

"Fucking bollocks."

She shook her head.

The former SAS operator continued, "Listen, the only way we'll get anything out of him is to give him something he really wants."

"I can't say I like your attitude," Fitzgerald said.

"Well, get used to it. Can I dangle the carrot or not?"

A nod. "Do it."

Knocker went back to the interrogation room. He looked at Halim, who sat quietly, waiting for him to speak. "I'm not going to give you the names. However, I can give you something else."

"What?"

"Your freedom."

That got his attention.

"You tell me what I want to know, and instead of

getting locked away in a hole for a very long time, you'll be put on a plane and sent back to Libya."

It took Halim a few moments to digest the information. "All right."

"What were you offered?"

"Money and weapons."

"Weapons from who? The Americans?"

He shook his head. "No. Not unless the US government is using Beretta ARX 160s."

"Italian weapons."

"Yes."

"How many?"

"Five hundred."

"And the money?"

"Ten million."

"Who for?"

"Me."

Knocker nodded again. "Thank you."

———

They stood in the room brainstorming ideas, but there was only one that made sense. "He's paying for it himself," Knocker said. "The weapons and money."

"But the question remains, where did the money and weapons come from?" Thurston said.

"Gun-runner," Kane theorized.

Fitzgerald shook his head. "How does a gun-runner become the head of National Intelligence?"

Knocker stared at him. "How does a member of the Cabal become President?"

"What?"

"That one hasn't reached this side of the pond?"

Knocker asked. "Carter was Numero Uno in the Cabal until they killed him."

The head of MI5 glanced at Thurston, who said, "It's true."

"You know," Cara said, "he just could be Cabal."

"I thought all that ended with Ellen Grayson?" Fitzgerald asked.

"They had to get their weapons from somewhere. Maybe he's branched out on his own."

"That's a long stretch." The MI5 commander scoffed.

"Then we need to find out. Those weapons had to come from somewhere," Ferrero said.

"Let Slick run with it while he's looking for Finn."

"Yes, ma'am."

"You know what I think?" Knocker asked.

"What?" they all said in unison as they looked to him for his suggestion.

"I think we need to shake him up a bit."

"How?" Thurston asked.

"He knows what we can do. Let's give him a friendly warning."

"What do you mean?"

"Let me explain."

———

WASHINGTON, DC

The phone on Edison's desk rang twice before he picked it up with a manicured hand. "Edison."

"I'm coming for you, Edison."

"Kane? Is that you?" The intelligence officer waved

his hand to get the attention of anyone outside his glass bubble.

"Yeah, it's me."

Someone saw Edison and started the trace. "To what do I owe the pleasure?"

"You made a mistake when you went after my sister."

"She's a criminal."

"The second one you made was when you hired Libyans to come after my team," Kane continued.

The revelation made him think twice about a response. "I don't know what you're talking about."

"I think you do. But we've found a nice place for us here in Britain. You already know that, though."

"Private contractors. I see."

"Working for MI5 at the minute, tracking terrorists. You know, it's amazing what you can find when you start digging. Turn your television on."

Edison looked at the screen in the corner. He picked up the remote from his desk and turned it on. "So?"

"Find the BBC."

He switched to it and froze. He saw a picture of himself. The ticker along the bottom said that one Brett Edison, believed to be a United States citizen, was wanted for questioning for the illegal sale of weapons and transfer of money. He was also wanted for kidnapping and arms dealing with terrorist factions across the globe.

"What have you done?" he hissed.

"You're in our world now, Edison. The Reaper is coming."

The line disconnected.

Edison stared at the screen and felt his throat tighten. This was bad. Unbelievably bad.

———

Borden Hunt and Rucker followed Edison to a quiet location on the outskirts of Washington DC soon after the call from Kane. The two former SEALs had been put in place in case something like that happened.

The intelligence officer was meeting a big man with a bushy beard. He had close-cropped hair and a sleeve of tattoos on each arm. The two former SEALs had ditched their ride and made their way through thick shrubbery to watch through binoculars.

"I've seen this guy before," Hunt said. He was of average height and build, with dark hair. He was at the top of his profession, whatever that now entailed. Rucker was a trained combat medic and stood a hair over six feet. The men had served together for the past few years and were the go-to guys for Alex Joseph when shit hit the fan.

"Who do you think he is?" Rucker asked.

"Bear Travis."

"The bounty hunter?"

Hunt nodded. "What do you figure he's up to?"

Bear Travis had once been a Ranger sergeant with tours all over the world. Now he was a bounty hunter in charge of a six-person team. He'd been known to operate across the globe in different war zones for the intelligence community, accepting jobs that only merce-naries could perform. As such, he was wanted in four countries for suspicious practices, mainly torturing and shooting prisoners.

"It seems mighty coincidental that he gets a call from Kane and then comes here. He's sending him after Kane."

"My thoughts exactly."

Rucker chuckled.

"Is something funny?"

"Yeah. I've never seen a bear who bit off more than he could chew."

"You're about to. Come on, let's report in."

———

"You want me to go after them all or just Kane?" Bear asked.

"The team. The five of them."

The big man nodded. "How much?"

"Ten million."

Bear let out a low whistle. "Big money."

"Don't underestimate them. They're good."

"From what I've heard, they're better than good. So is their commander."

"Thurston?"

"Yeah. The general is one hell of a leader."

"Is there going to be a problem, Bear?"

"Has there ever been?"

"Just as long as we don't have one now."

"There won't be," he replied in a guttural growl. "Where are they?"

"London, England."

"What are they doing there?"

"Hiding from me."

"Does this have anything to do with Kane's sister?" Bear asked.

"How—"

"I hear things, Edison. I'll tell you this; you've sure got a tiger by the tail."

"Can you fix it or not?"

"I'll fix it. But the ten million you're paying me is up front. I want another ten when it's done."

"What?"

"Take it or leave it," the big man said. "I'm going to lose people on this mission. It takes money to train them."

"Alright but understand this. If I'm paying this much money, I expect results."

"You'll get them."

———

LONDON, ENGLAND

"What do we know about the bomb outside the Mountbatten?" Thurston asked.

Swift put up a video feed on the big screen. "This is the lorry used to deliver the bomb. *That* is the driver getting out."

"Can we get a closer look at it?" Kane asked.

"Sure."

The picture zoomed in, and he got to see the face of Kyran Finn. "Son of a bitch."

The camera rolled some more. Swift paused it as a woman with a young child walked past the lorry. They were the closest. There were pedestrians coming the other way too. "Not long after this, the bomb exploded."

"The woman and the little girl?" Cara asked, already knowing the answer.

Swift shook his head.

A heavy silence descended on the room.

"Where did he go?" Kane asked.

"I was able to track his movements to a house in Willesden Green. The address belongs to a Daniel O'Donnell. One-time IRA supporter who now supposedly keeps his nose clean."

"Not so much by the looks of that," Axe said. "Is the target still in the building?"

"You make it sound like we're going after him," Thurston remarked.

"Aren't we?"

"Yes, I suppose you are."

"Tonight?"

"No, as soon as possible. We'll coordinate with MI5 and the Met. They'll block off the street while you go in."

"Rules of engagement?" Brick asked.

"You're in a friendly environment. Try not to kill anyone. You'll go in with beanbag rounds."

"I'll do that," Axe said. "Won't be needing a SAW this time out."

Thurston nodded. "Gear up."

WILLESDEN GREEN, LONDON

They rolled up in two armored Range Rovers. One was driven by Troy, the other by Traynor. This was to free the team up so they could climb out of the vehicles immediately without any impediments.

Down the street, the teams pulled up outside a

yellow-painted brick abode that mirrored all those adjoining it. Every dwelling was attached to the one next door.

The five operators emerged from the vehicles and moved with practiced ease through the open gate in the red-brick fence and up the short path to the front door.

They stopped on either side of the door. Standing in front of it with a possible shooter on the other side was never a wise move.

Knocker stepped forward with a breaching gun, which was actually a shotgun, and blew off the lock.

Axe, with his bean bag gun, was first in. He walked through the hall and past the stairs that led up to the second floor. Brick stopped at the foot of the stairs and kept his M6 trained up the steep incline.

Axe kept going, sweeping each room as he went. Once he was sure all was clear, he backtracked and went up the stairs, with Brick behind him.

The bedroom on the left at the top was clear. The one on the right had two bodies in it. Both were naked, a man and a woman. Shot in the head.

Axe finished his sweep, came back to the bedroom, and found Kane and Cara there. The Team Reaper commander looked up and asked, "Nothing?"

Axe shook his head. "No sign."

"How the hell did he get out? Search this place from top to bottom."

"Roger that."

"That's our guy," Cara said. "But I wonder who the woman is?"

Kane took out his cell phone and captured a photo. "Slick, I'm sending something your way. See if you can ID the woman."

"Copy, Reaper."

"Zero, our target is dead, and so is his companion. No sign of Kyran Finn."

"Copy, Reaper. Keep us updated."

Kane muttered a curse under his breath. He started to look around the room for anything that might help ID the woman. There was plenty to confirm the identity of the male, but it looked as though the woman's ID had been taken.

"Reaper, you need to see this," Knocker said.

"Where are you?"

"The second bedroom."

Kane and Cara went across the hallway and found Knocker. He was staring at the wall adjoining the house next door. "Notice anything about the room?"

Kane frowned as he looked around. "Is it smaller?"

"That's what I thought, so I stepped it out. I was right. Then I moved the wardrobe." He showed them how it swiveled on a hinge. Kane was impressed. "It's like a panic room, except it isn't."

Through the opening was another room. This one took up what was left of the room they were in and part of the one next door. It also had a doorway. They walked inside. The walls were adorned with automatic weapons as well as handguns. A table sat in the corner, with a security camera system set up. Knocker said, "I wouldn't touch anything if I were you. We found something like this in Belfast some years back, and it was booby-trapped. The poor sod who was left to keep an eye on it blew himself up when he started fiddling with it."

The Brit checked the opposite doorway, then pushed it open. On the other side was a bedroom, this one markedly different from the one they'd just left. It was a little girl's room, complete with dolls and toys.

"Bravo Four, I need a full intel package on the people who live in Forty-Six."

"Roger that."

"Look at this, Reaper."

Kane turned to see Cara holding out a frame with a picture inside. It was of a little girl with her mother. Cara said, "I gather she's a single mom."

"Looks that way." His brow furrowed as he studied the little girl's face. He pressed his transmit button and said, "Bravo Four, can you find out if Kyran Finn has a kid? A girl. She looks to be six, I'd say."

"Wait one, Reaper."

Cara studied the little girl's face. "I can't believe I didn't see it sooner."

He nodded. "Search the house. Let's find all we can."

CHAPTER 14

WILLESDEN GREEN, LONDON

"IT'S DEFINITELY JUST the woman and her kid," Knocker said. "We've been over this place with a fine-tooth comb and found nothing to say otherwise. The daughter, Kaitlin, goes to the local school down the road. The mother's name is Meara. Their surname is Carroll."

"No photos of the father?"

"Not one. It's like she's gone out of her way to keep him out of their lives."

Kane said, "Maybe she didn't want the daughter to know who her father was. But why all the hardware?"

"Still one with the cause, I suppose."

"It doesn't make sense."

"Never does."

"Reaper One, copy?"

"Go ahead, Bravo Four."

"I have some information on your resident. Meara Carroll lived in Belfast before moving to London six years ago. There is no mention of a child, but I'd say she was pregnant at the time. She was known to be with Kyran Finn for twelve months before moving. MI5 had a watch on her early, but nothing came of it."

"Well, she's not retired. Either that or she's being used. We need to see if anyone has left the building."

"Already done. I found a woman, her child, and a male wearing a hoodie leaving in a red Volvo. Couldn't make out the man's face, but it seems the woman and child were reluctant to leave."

Cara couldn't understand it. Here was a woman sharing a weapons cache with a man, yet...

"Could having the baby have changed her outlook on life?"

"Most probably."

"Whoa," said Swift over the comms. "I wasn't expecting that."

"Expecting what?" Kane asked.

"The dead woman in the bed with Daniel O'Donnell is Meara Carroll."

"He killed the mother and took the kid," Cara said. "The question is, who is the woman that went with him?"

Kane's face hardened. "Slick, find that damned car."

"On it."

———

Kaitlin sobbed quietly in the rear seat of the Volvo. She knew enough to realize her mother was dead. She'd gleaned that from the way Missy was arguing with the man who claimed to be her father.

"What is wrong with you, you fucking gobshite?" Missy growled. "You go and—"

"Just shut the fuck up," Kyran snarled. "Let me think."

"Your fucking da will take your shitting head off your shoulders."

"I just wanted to see her before I had to disappear," Kyran reasoned.

"Disappear from what?"

"I can't say."

"It was you, wasn't it?" Missy asked as the penny dropped. "That bomb today was you."

"Not just me."

"Jesus H. Christ. Are you trying to start another war with the Brits?"

"It's for the good of the cause."

"Fuck the cause," she spat. "Is it worth all the innocents dying?"

"There was a time when you would have been up there leading the charge, Missy," Kyran pointed out.

"That was another life."

"Just drive, Missy. And keep off the main roads."

"Where are we going?"

"I'll tell you when we get there. Just drive."

Missy looked in the rearview mirror. "Are you all right, honey?"

"I want to go home," Kaitlin sobbed.

"I know, sweetie. Real soon. After we fix this thing with Grandda."

"I don't have a grandda."

"You see?" Kyran snarled. "You see what the bitch did?"

"Oh, fucking grow up, Kyran. You were a right prick, and you know it."

"Watch your mouth, Missy, or you'll get the same."

"Shit, if I had a dick, you could go suck it." Missy's anger was taking over, and she'd had enough. She'd arrived just after Kyran had killed her friend, and he'd forced her to drive him wherever he wanted to go.

"Just shut up, Missy," he snapped. "Turn right here."

"How much further?"

"Not far."

"Is your da going to be there?"

"Just drive."

———

"Do you have him yet?" Ferrero asked.

"The car has stopped at an apartment complex in an unsavory part of London," Swift explained.

"What?"

"It's run by an Irish gang called the Leprechauns."

Ferrero sighed. "Original."

"What they do isn't so much. They're headed by a man named Fogarty. He runs an import-export business. They import drugs and export money back to Dublin. Once there, all funds go into the bank account of Rory Miller."

"Who's he when he's at home?"

"He's the head Leprechaun. Kind of like the head of a Mexican cartel, only it's Irish. Word is he's worth two hundred million."

"That's not much."

"That's his clean money. He's got other stuff in

foreign banks, assets, hidden cash deposits, art works, and so on and so on. All up into the billions. A Hong Kong triad was working the Projects before the Irish moved in a few years ago. The Irish cleaned them out."

"Why would Kyran go there?" Ferrero asked.

"He and Fogarty go back a ways. Grew up together."

"So he's looking for a place to hide?"

"That would be my guess."

"Well, get me all you can. We're going to have to get him out of there."

"Roger that."

Ferrero switched his mike on. "Reaper One, copy?"

"Read you Lima Charlie, Zero."

"Listen, we've got a location on your target. He's holed up in a housing project run by what Slick described as the Irish Mafia. Expect a hostile welcome."

"Rules of engagement?"

"It's a public housing estate. The last thing we want is a firefight on the streets. Use your discretion, but no, I repeat, no civilian casualties if it can be helped. Have Traynor and Troy RTB, over."

"Roger that. Out."

———

"Fuck me," Knocker said as he looked up from within the SUV. "This thing is a death trap. All twenty sodding floors of it."

The Brit's description of the high-rise apartment complex was exaggerated by two floors. The actual height of it was eighteen stories. He looked at Kane. "Who is the cock that's running this shitshow?"

"Someone named Fogarty," Kane replied.

"It would be," the Brit groaned. "I had me a bad feeling, and now it's come true. Let's just sod off to the pub. My shout."

"You know this asshole?" Axe asked. "What's he like?"

"Axel, me old mate, I'd rather run naked between two rows of horny fifty-something housewives than go in there."

"You what?"

"Don't worry."

"How many men would he have, Knocker?" Cara asked.

"Thirty or forty?"

"Piss off," Brick growled.

"Mate, I shit you not. That place is loaded with pricks who want nothing more than to make a name for themselves."

Kane pressed his transmit button. "Bravo Four, I need to know how many stairwells in this place. Over."

"Two, Reaper. North and south."

"Can you shut the elevators down?"

"Not remotely, but I can cut the power."

"Do it."

"On it."

"What floor are we expecting this guy to be on?"

"Sixteenth."

Kane looked at Cara. "I'll give you Knocker and Brick. I'll take Axe with me. You get the south stairwell; I'll take north. We go up hard. Secure the floor, and once we have the package in hand, we reassess and go from there."

"Roger that."

Kane pressed his talk button to reach out to the second vehicle. "Axe, Brick, we're moving. Axe with me. Brick, you're with Cara and Knocker. Go now."

The doors on the vehicles opened, and they all emerged in tactical gear and carrying suppressed M6s. They split as they crossed the parking lot, headed for the doors at either end of the rectangular concrete building.

"Bravo Four, I need real-time updates on all activity, over."

"You'll get it, Reaper One."

"All right, people. Let's do this."

———

"Hello, there," Cara said as she held the suppressor about six inches from the Irishman's nose. "Why don't you and your mate get on your knees? There's a good chap."

"Spoken like a true Brit, ma'am. Your accent could do with some work, though," Knocker told her as he tied the two men's hands behind their backs with zip-ties. He checked under their jackets and came out with two handguns. He smacked one on the back of his head. "Stupid twat. Don't you know you shouldn't play with guns?"

"Fuck off," the Irishmen spat.

Knocker hit him again.

"Is your boss home today?"

"Screw you."

The Brit knocked him out with his next blow. He then looked at the second Irishman. "What about you?"

"He's there."

Brick knocked him out as well.

"Reaper One, be advised package two is in the building," Cara said, informing Kane that Fogarty was home.

"Roger that. Entering now."

The inside of the stairwell smelled of stale urine. The carpet was dirty, and the tiles were marked. The walls had graffiti painted on them, one tag belonging to someone named Ed.

They moved through the empty foyer toward a door marked with the word *Stairs*. Cara reached out to turn the knob when Kane's voice came over the comms. "Contact...shit."

The distant rattle of gunfire came through the building. Cara said into her comms, "Reaper, are you alright?"

"We're fine. Just keep pushing up."

"Roger that."

Cara started up the stairwell, Knocker behind her, then Brick. The gunfire they'd heard had ceased and been replaced by voices. They reached the first floor and kept climbing. Somewhere above them, a door slammed, and footsteps could be heard clattering on the stairs.

Cara had the M6 at her shoulder, pointing upward. Three men appeared, all armed with various weapons. They saw Cara and froze. She spoke in a calm voice. "Put the guns down, and we'll all get along just fine."

Two considered it, but the third was twitchy. There was always a twitchy guy.

He muttered a curse and brought up his weapon. Cara shot him twice, and he jerked and died. The two with him lost control of what they were doing and went the same way as their partner.

Cara shifted her aim and shot the second one in the chest. The third was killed by Knocker. A bullet to the brain will do that to you. The brass from their bullets tinkled as it hit the hard stairs, the sound echoing throughout the stairwell.

The second man to be shot started to slither down the stairs toward them like some macabre snake. Cara ignored him and climbed higher.

Once more, gunfire rang out from the other stairwell. This time it was more intense. Behind Cara, Knocker said, "I knew this was a bad idea. So much shit going down, and we haven't even reached the third floor yet."

———

Gunfire shattered the quiet of the stairwell, and Kane met it with a volley of his own. He ducked back, and Axe let loose with a burst up the center opening at a head peering over the side. The person disappeared after a round snapped their head back. The weapon they were holding fell through the opening between the rails to the ground floor. "So much for doing this the easy way," Axe growled as he dropped out a magazine and replaced it with a fresh one. "The way we're going, I'll be out of ammo before we reach the tenth floor."

Kane looked at the door beside him. It would take him into the hallway that serviced the fourth floor. From there, they could cross to the other stairwell and continue up. However, it would leave this one unprotected and open.

Kane flipped the selector to auto and sent up another burst of gunfire, then replaced the spent magazine. "Put it on semi, Axe, and follow me."

Kane raised his carbine and started up the stairs. More gunfire came at them, but he ignored it as he fired two shots at another Leprechaun. The man dropped and didn't move again. Kane and Axe stepped over him as they continued their climb, pushing their attackers back. Stopping on five, they reloaded again. Axe said, "How are we supposed to get to the right floor like this? We need to pull back and rethink."

Kane stared at him. He was right. "Reaper Two, sitrep, over."

"Reaper, we've reached six, but we're taking heavy fire."

"Roger that. Pull back to five, over."

"Copy."

"Zero, copy?"

"I've got you, Reaper," Ferrero answered.

"There's no way we can reach our target this way."

"All right, Reaper. Regroup and get out of there."

Kane relayed the message to Cara, and they pulled back. Once out of the building, they hurried across the lot to the waiting vehicles. It wasn't until they'd covered half the distance that Brick shouted, "RPG!"

As one, the team flattened on the asphalt-covered lot. The rocket-propelled grenade streaked overhead and smashed into the first of the armored SUVs the team had arrived in. A great fireball erupted and rose into the air. Shards of debris rained down.

"Where'd that come from?" Kane called.

"Tenth floor, far-right window," Brick said loudly, his ears still ringing.

"Put some fire on it."

Before anyone could respond, another rocket-propelled grenade tore across the gap from the window to the second SUV. The result was the same.

Kane shook his head. "Zero, this is Reaper One. We're taking RPG fire and have lost our transport." Behind him, the others started to pepper the window from which the RPG had been fired. "We need extract, over."

"I'll see what I can do. Dig in, Reaper. It could be a while."

"Great."

"Police are responding."

"No, keep them back. They'll just walk into a shitstorm."

"Roger that. Out."

Kane looked around and saw an apartment complex across the way that appeared abandoned. It was a single-level building, much like a motel. "Cara, over there. We hole up until help arrives."

She nodded. "Let's do it."

She led out on point. Bullets hit the ground around the team as they ran. Kane heard Knocker say something but wasn't sure what it was. "Say again."

"I said, this is a right royal cockup."

"You mean it's fucked, right?" Axe asked.

"Sideways, me old mate. It's fucked sideways."

The sound of snapping bullets was never a good thing, especially when it was happening at regular intervals. The team leaped over a low brick fence and crouched behind it. Brick and Knocker looked for targets of opportunity and began shooting back. They were joined by Cara, who emptied a magazine at two shooters who had taken shelter behind a large dumpster.

"They're gathering thick and fast," she said, changing out an empty magazine.

"Welcome to the latest conflict zone," Knocker said. "London's Irish Projects, the only place you can go to shoot Leprechauns."

"You should put that on a tourist brochure," Cara said, rising and firing once more.

"By the time it takes off, all the Leprechauns will be gone, ma'am," the Brit said as he watched another shooter fall.

"Good point."

Kane said, "Knocker, Cara, you've got our six. We'll pull back to the apartment complex. Once we're there, we'll cover you."

"Roger that."

The three of them fell back until they reached the complex. Kane kicked open the first door they came to, and they went inside. The place was empty, complete with holes in walls and graffiti to boot. It stank of damp. Kane figured the brick exterior would be a bonus for incoming rounds. "Brick, check the back door."

"On it."

Axe looked around the room, smiling. "I like the new digs. Artwork on every wall. Smells a bit funky, though."

Kane pressed his talk button. "Cara, come to us."

"On our way."

Kane and Axe gave them cover fire as they ran the rest of the way. But instead of coming into the apartment Kane and the others were in, they hit the one next door. Cara's voice came over the comms. "We're good, Reaper."

"Check the back door, Reaper Two."

"All taken care of."

Brick appeared. "Nothing out the back except a brick wall, Reaper. It's a shit field of vision. They could sneak up on us from there, and we would not see them coming until it was too late."

"Let's hope they're not that smart." Kane looked out the window Axe had knocked out for safety. The Leprechauns had stopped firing, which meant they were up to something. "Keep an eye out, people. All we've got to do now is hang on until the cavalry arrives."

CHAPTER 15

LONDON, ENGLAND

"THE MET HAS SEALED off the Projects and is holding about a mile from Ground Zero, Mary," Ferrero told Thurston as she studied the screen receiving the feed from the UAV above.

"Where are they?" she asked, not shifting her gaze.

"In the apartment complex to the right. Their main problem is going to be ammunition."

"And there is no way of getting any into them." She said it as a statement rather than a question.

"Not at this point. Which wouldn't matter anyway because if we could get to them, then we could get them out."

"Where are we on help?"

"Global is sending in a team by chopper. Should be here within the hour."

"It'll be dark by then."

"Yes, ma'am."

Thurston frowned. "Where are they going to land?"

"That's the other problem," Ferrero explained. He pointed at a map on the desk beside him. "There is a football field here. It's five hundred meters from the place where the team is holed up. They'll fight their way in and then out while both choppers hold in the air until extract."

"Size of the team?"

"Six."

"Is that all?"

"That's it," Ferrero confirmed.

"Who is their team leader?" Thurston asked.

"An old friend from Helmand. Former Marine Commando Sergeant Richard Todd."

Thurston gave a nod of satisfaction. "Let's hope it all works out. What's their call sign?"

"His is King One. The chopper, Talisman Zero-One."

"Let Kane know."

"Yes, ma'am."

Thurston's cell rang. "Thurston."

"Mary, what's the score?" Hank Jones asked.

"The team is pinned down, but they're all still in good shape. I'm guessing you know about the incoming help?"

"Yes, I do, seeing as I was the one who signed off on it."

"Thank you, sir."

"Tell me what happened."

She ran through the short version, and once she'd finished, Jones said, "Keep me up to date on events, Mary."

It was his way of letting her know he wasn't happy about finding out about the situation the way he had.

"Roger that, sir."

No sooner had Thurston hung up than her cell rang again. "Shit. Thurston."

"Mary, Fitzgerald."

"Make it brief. I'm kind of busy." She winced. She hadn't meant to sound so abrupt. "Sorry, Frank."

"It's all right. I've got the prime minister breathing down my neck, trying to find out what's going on."

"I've got a team pinned down and another coming in to help extract them. They are surrounded in the Projects by Leprechauns."

"Little—"

"Not funny, Frank. They've got automatic weapons and RPGs."

"Sorry. It sounds like Syria, not London."

"It might as well be. How do these guys get a hold like this?"

"Over time. The Projects is a housing commission part of London. You know, public housing supplied by the government."

"Uh-huh."

"Once they give them a roof, they don't give bollocks about the rest. The criminal element moves in, law and order move out."

"I've seen it before."

"What do I tell the prime minister?"

"Tell him to get his shit together."

"All right."

"Wait," Mary corrected. "Tell him the situation is fluid."

"I'll do that."

The call disconnected, and Thurston swore. She

looked at the large screen and saw that the sun was almost gone. She said, "Teller, put up infrared."

The screen changed, and the feed from the UAV took a disturbing turn. "Pete, make it clear. What am I looking at?"

"In the center of the screen is the team, ma'am. The rest of the dots, except for the larger ones, are bad news."

"I was afraid of that."

As she stared at the screen, she did a mental calculation. They were facing a small army, one that was closing in and tightening the noose.

"We need to get them out of there."

———

ABOARD TALISMAN ZERO-ONE, OVER LONDON

"Two minutes!" The words sounded distant with the noise of the Chinook beating in his ears. Former Sergeant Richard Todd changed his comms channel and repeated them to his team. He then rechecked his equipment, starting with his M6. The ramp at the rear of the helicopter was partially down, and he could see the darkness outside. Each of the King team had night-vision goggles attached to their ballistic helmets, should they be required.

Although he felt a little apprehensive about the mission, he knew that once he stepped off the ramp, old habits would kick in, and it would be business as usual. In one way, he was pleased he could repay the favor to the people who'd saved him and his team in Afghanistan.[1]

The pitch of the Chinook changed, and he felt the helicopter start to drop. The ramp at the rear lowered more without going all the way down. The crew chief gave him the signal for thirty seconds.

He repeated it to his men, and moments later, the Chinook rocked as its wheels touched down. The ramp lowered the rest of the way and the team exited, taking a knee until the Chinook lifted off again and disappeared with its escort into the darkness of the London night.

Todd looked at his second in command, another former commando who'd gotten out after ten years, named Mike Roberts. Roberts was a big man who'd made it to regimental sergeant major. As tough as they came, he took no shit from anyone. The men all called him Robbo.

"Pick a man, Robbo," Todd said.

Roberts turned to the man nearest to him and said in his deep voice, "On point, Womble, there's a good lad."

Benny Hill and Crumpet Davies grinned at each other in the dark.

"And if you two pricks don't get them fucking smirks off your faces right now, I'm going to cut your cocks off and feed them to my ex-wife's terrier, shitting, fucking animal that it is."

"Yes, Robbo," they whispered.

"Or maybe I'll let her chew on them instead. Now there's a scary thought."

Todd grinned to himself at the words. Roberts may have been a big, scary NCO in his time, but his dry sense of humor was next level.

As Bollocks Walker eased past Roberts to fall in behind Womble Cooper, he said, "I'd rather be attached to mine if she's going to do it, Robbo. She's not half-bad, your ex-missus."

"Shut up and keep moving."

In the distance, a burst of gunfire could be heard. Todd said, "At least someone is still alive."

"This reminds me so much of Afghanistan that I have to keep reminding myself it's London."

"That's the sad part of it. These turnips are allowed to move in and take over, and no one gives a fuck. Let's go get our friends, Robbo."

They started moving toward the gunfire.

———

"I just saw a Chinook take off, Reaper," Brick said as he checked his ammo. "Could be our relief."

"Let's hope so." He pressed his talk button. "I need an ammo check from everyone."

One by one they called in, each repeating the same story. No one had more than two magazines left. However, they still had three magazines each for their sidearms. "All right. Single shots only, conserve your ammunition."

Sudden gunfire erupted from a position around seventy yards out. Tracers ripped through the darkness and punched into the crumbling brickwork of the apartment Cara and Knocker were in. "Where the frig did those guys get tracer rounds from?" Cara growled as she hunkered down, trying to protect herself from the rounds coming through the exposed wall.

"Probably the same place they got the RPGs," Knocker replied.

"Reaper, can you get a shot at this asshole?"

"Wait one."

After a few moments, the firing stopped, and Axe said, "Lights out, ma'am."

"Thanks, Axe."

"Contact rear!" Brick's voice was urgent.

Knocker came to his feet and ran to the rear of the apartment. At the back, there was a narrow lane between the building and the brick wall, and it seemed that the Leprechauns had worked out that they could use the wall to their advantage. The Brit had just entered the room when something round and heavy bounced through the window, smashing as it went.

Knocker's eyes widened when he realized that it was a grenade and it had stopped a few feet away. Although he couldn't see it, he just knew.

"Shit!" he growled and dove back into the opening he'd just come through.

The explosion ripped the room apart, blowing holes in the wall and showering Knocker with debris. He coughed and tasted blood in his mouth. "Cock," he mumbled.

Cara appeared above him. "You alright?"

"Never better."

She helped him up and dragged him to the other room. "Keep an eye out front," she said and moved toward the back room.

"Cara, are you alright?" Kane asked over the comms.

"We're good."

"What was that explosion?"

"Grenade."

She checked the alley out the back and saw that there were three dark shapes lying on the ground. "We all clear back here, Brick?"

"As clear as we can be."

"Roger that."

She went back to the front of the apartment and found Knocker watching out the window. "What's happening?"

"Things have quieted down. I'd say that they were the diversion to distract us from the attack on the back."

"Are you feeling alright?"

"Good as gold."

"No blurred vision, headaches?"

"I'm good, Cara."

"Fine."

———

Todd hunkered down next to Womble and asked, "What's the problem?"

They had pushed forward, using force where necessary. They'd taken down five shooters so far and were maybe a hundred meters from the apartment complex where Reaper and his team were holed up.

Womble said, "I've got another armed tango ahead of us."

"Well, fix the problem."

"It's a woman."

"Give me a look."

Todd pushed in beside his man and through his

NVGs, he could see that Womble was right. It was a woman, and she was armed with an AK. Todd drew back. "All right, we'll go around."

They changed direction and went around another taller apartment block. "Damn it," Womble groaned.

"What is it?"

"Got another couple outriders."

Todd eased his way up to where Womble was kneeling, his sights locked onto one of the targets. The team leader had a look and said, "Hold fire, Womble."

"Aye."

"Reaper One, this is King One, copy?" Todd's voice wasn't much more than a whisper.

"Copy, King One, read you Lima Charlie."

"Reaper, we're on our way in from the east. There are six of us. Hold your fire."

"Come on in. Watch out to the west."

"Roger that." Todd turned to Womble. "Let's drop these scousers."

They brought their weapons up and picked their targets. Todd breathed out slowly and said, "Execute."

They both squeezed the triggers on their M6s, and the two outriders dropped. "All right, let's do this."

———

Fogarty ran a hand through his red hair and glared at his friend. "You brought this shite to me, Kyran. The boss is going to be over the fucking moon about it."

"How was I to know they would come here? All I needed was a place to lay low while the heat cooled down."

"And you brought the bitch and the kid."

"The kid is mine."

Missy watched them warily. One word, and she knew the unstable pair would kill her. She hugged the little girl to her.

"Meanwhile, I'm losing people hand over fist, and I've got military on our turf. If we ever get out of this, I'm going to have to go to ground. Not from the fucking coppers but from frigging Rory. He'll kill me at the drop of a hat."

"What are you going to do? I paid you to come here."

"Worst mistake I ever made. Well, we need to get out of here while it's still dark."

The cell in Fogarty's pocket rang. He took it out and looked at the number. "Fuck," he growled.

"What?"

"It's him."

"Him who?"

"Who do you reckon, you dick? It sure isn't the Queen of fucking England."

"Rory?"

Fogarty rolled his eyes and answered the cell. "Rory, listen, I—"

He stopped and listened. "I can't do that. He's my—"

More listening.

Kyran was suddenly on edge, and his hand slipped behind his back to his gun. Fogarty finished the call and looked at his friend. He shrugged.

"Is everything alright?" Kyran asked.

"I'm sorry, man."

Kyran nodded, drew his gun, and shot him in the chest.

Missy gave a yelp of surprise. "What did you do?"

"He was going to kill me. Now bring the kid; we're getting out of here."

"You're crazy."

"Just do it," he roared. "We're leaving, now."

———

"Good to see you, Rich," Kane said. "Didn't know you were with Global."

"You too, Reaper. Yeah, I got out and came to work for the man. Got a good team, too. Robbo here is as good a second dickie as they come."

Kane looked at the big man through the gloom. "Robbo."

He muttered something and wandered off. Todd said, "He'll warm up to you. Typical company sergeant major. Fights like a bull, though."

"I'd hate to meet him in a dark alley."

"Join the club. What have we got?"

"Cara and Knocker are in the apartment next door—"

Todd said into his comms, "Crumpet, Benny, next door."

"On it, Boss."

Kane continued, "They tried to get in here a couple of times but were shit out of luck. Thing is, they've got tracers, machine guns, and RPGs."

"We took a few out on the way in, but if we're to get out, now is probably the time."

"Reaper, we've got movement," Swift said into his comms.

"What's going on, Bravo Four?"

"They're pulling back."

"Who? The Leprechauns?"

"Yes, they're all disappearing off the screen."

"What about in the target building?"

"Looks like they're abandoning it."

Kane looked at Todd. "They're pulling out. Time to look in that building."

"Show me the way."

———

They didn't worry about sweeping the floors as they went. There was no need. The building was empty.

They found Fogarty where he'd been left dead on the floor. Kane said, "Looks like there was a falling out between friends."

"It would explain why everyone left," Cara said.

Kane picked up the cell from the floor. "Slick can work his magic on this."

Brick appeared. "There's no sign of the girl, the woman, or Kyran Finn."

Cara pressed her talk button. "Bravo Four, copy?"

"I'm still here, ma'am."

"There's no sign of the target or his hostages. We think he slipped out after killing his host."

"I'll see what I can find, ma'am."

"Roger that. Out." She looked at Kane. "The blood hound is on the case."

"Let's hope he can find something."

Todd paused then said, "Copy, Crumpet."

"What's up?"

"The Met has arrived with their armed response boys."

"Good," said Kane. "Let's get this over and done with. I'm ready for some shuteye."

---

1. See *Collateral Damage*

CHAPTER 16

SOMEWHERE IN THE NORTH OF ENGLAND

BRIAN FINN WAS ANGRY. Sure, the bombing had gone to plan, but Kyran was missing when he was supposed to have returned to the prearranged rendezvous so they could all leave England together. He looked up as O'Connor entered the study, the warmth from the fire escaping out the dark-stained solid wood door.

"What's the gobshite done now?" Finn asked as he saw the expression on the enforcer's face.

"I reached out to some friends, but it seems that the boy has gone a touch too far this time around."

"Just fucking tell me," Finn snarled.

"He went to Meara's place."

"To see Kaitlin?"

O'Connor nodded. "Something happened. He killed her and took the girl. Took Missy, too."

"Fuck me."

"That's not all."

"It never is."

"He went to the Projects."

"Where that wanker of a friend of his is?"

"Yes. The problem was, he was found by the team from Global. Fogarty declared open war on them and got his ass kicked. Rory Miller got wind of it and ordered Fogarty to kill Kyran. Seems that Kyran beat him to the punch."

"Damn that boy."

"What do you want me to do? Miller will still have a kill order on him, and everyone is looking for him. Then there's the kid."

Finn was torn, and the expression on his face said as much. He'd done all he could to make his son right, yet there was always something. Now, he'd screwed everything up. "Can I trust you to take care of it, Braden?"

"Are you sure?" O'Connor asked deadpan.

"Yes. If I don't, then Miller will."

"I could always kill Rory Miller."

"No, it's better this way."

"What about the girl?"

"No, leave her unharmed. It's not her fault her da was a dope. Do you know where he is?"

"I have an idea."

"Once it's done, we'll leave."

"All right, I'll go now."

After he'd left the study, Keira entered. "What was that I overheard?"

"Something about your brother," he mumbled.

"What's he done now?"

"Don't worry about it."

She looked at him, concerned. "Tell me, Da. You've

dragged me away from my home to here, done God only knows what, and you've told me fuck all."

"Keira—"

"No, Da, enough is enough."

"All right, but remember, you asked."

"Da—"

"He killed Meara and took the girl."

"What? No." Keira's face crumpled, and she placed her hands over her mouth.

"I'm sorry, Keira, it's true. Rory Miller has put a hit on him."

"We have to find him and Kaitlin before he does."

Finn slowly shook his head. "No, Keira."

"What do you mean, no?" She stood with her hands on hips, ready to defy him.

"I've told Braden to take care of it."

She gave him a questioning look before realization hit. "Oh, Da, no. He's your son."

"It's me or Miller, Keira. The boy is out of control."

"Just like you with your bombs and other bullshit."

"It's for the cause," he growled. "What he did was sheer bloody murder. Killing the girl's mother."

"I want Kaitlin with me."

He stared at his daughter. "Keira..."

"She's family, Da. I want to look after her."

"All right, I'll let Braden know."

"I'll never forgive you for this," she hissed. "Your own fucking son."

———

LONDON, ENGLAND

Kane got out of the shower, and after drying off, got half-dressed, leaving his shirt off. Cara sat on the bed in her panties and a tank top. Her hair was still wet. "Feel better?"

They'd slept most of the day, and now the sun was gone once more. "A little more human."

"Good."

There was a knock on the door, and Kane wandered over and opened it. On the other side stood a smiling Brit holding a six-pack of beer in his right hand. "Bloody hell, if I'd have known clothing was optional, I'd have come prepared."

Kane said, "Leave the beer and piss off."

"Nice try," Knocker said.

"Let him in, Reaper," Cara called. "He's got beer."

"You're lucky," Kane said, giving him a mock glare and stepping aside.

Knocker tossed Cara a beer, and as she cracked it, she gave the Brit a smile. "I think I love you, Knocker."

"I have that effect of the ladies." He grinned. "Besides the obvious, what are you all up to?"

"What do you mean, obvious?" Kane growled.

"You want me to spell it out?"

"No, please don't," Cara said. "We're just winding down."

"And that is why I brought beer."

Another knock on the door.

"What the hell is this, Grand Central Station?" Kane growled.

"Hey, Reaper, open the damn door."

Cara rolled her eyes. "Axe."

Kane opened the door, and both Axe and Brick stood there. Like Knocker, they both had beer. The team leader sighed. "Come on in."

"They better have beer," Cara called.

"Would we have anything else?" Brick asked.

Kane stood and looked at his team. "All right, what's going on?"

Brick said, "Does there have to be something going on?"

Knuckles on the door.

"What the hell is this?" Kane asked.

When he opened the door, Thurston, Arenas, and Ferrero stood there, holding even more beer. They pushed past him.

"Come on in," he said with more than a hint of sarcasm.

"Have you started yet?" Thurston asked.

"Not yet," Cara said.

Kane frowned as he looked at her. "You're part of this?"

"Maybe just a little bit," she allowed, holding up her thumb and forefinger, showing a little gap.

"Well?" Kane asked.

"We know that as soon as you get the chance, you're going to disappear and go after your sister," Ferrero said. "So, this is where we make a plan, and you don't have to do it on your own."

"Just wait—"

"Shut up," Knocker growled. "She's your family, she's our family. No one gets left behind."

"But we do have other issues," Thurston said.

"Like what?"

"Edison has hired Bear Travis to come after you, maybe us."

"So?"

"He's in London," Ferrero said. "Arrived a couple hours ago."

"Do we know where he is?"

"We do."

"Then we should go pay him a visit and take it to him."

"All right, I'll sign off on that."

"The other thing is getting into the US," Arenas said. "I have a cousin who will be able to get you in through Mexico."

Kane nodded. "All right."

Axe said, "By you, he means all of us, Reaper. You're not going on your own."

"I can accept that."

"First though, we have to deal with everything here. Understand?" Thurston said.

"Yes, ma'am."

She sighed. "Well, that was painless."

"Let's gear up and go—"

"Whoa, whoa, whoa," Knocker said. "Tonight, we drink beer, and we go pay this Bear cock a visit tomorrow."

"That's an order," Thurston confirmed.

"What about Kyran Finn?" Kane asked.

"MI5 is chasing that one for the moment. Fitzgerald wants us to have some downtime since we've been hard at it for a while."

"Fine," said Kane. "Let's go after Bear Travis and his people tomorrow."

———

"Are we sure they're in there?" Kane asked.

"They're there, all right."

Kane nodded and started to climb out of the SUV. "Well, I'd best go and pay him a visit. Is everyone in place?"

"They sure are," Cara confirmed.

"Then there's nothing else left to do." He then said into his comms, "Reaper One, moving."

Walking across the street, he approached a small rundown laundromat—just the type of place one would hide out with mercenaries. He stepped up to and through the front door, heading straight for the counter. A round man with wispy hair looked at him and said, "What can I do for you, chum?"

"I'm here to see Bear Travis."

"Who?"

"Bear Travis. Big guy with a shaved head and a bushy beard. Should be here with a group of other assholes."

"Don't know who you're talking about," Wispy said, bending down behind the counter.

The Glock came free of Kane's pants in one smooth movement. Before the guy behind the counter knew it, he was staring into the muzzle. "Come up nice and slow, or I'll give you a third eye."

"Whoa, mate, I wasn't doing anything." He raised his hands to shoulder height.

Kane stepped around the counter and grabbed Wispy by the collar. "All right, let's go see Bear."

They went through the door to the back, where the

machines worked noisily, doing what they were designed to do. Bursts of steam erupted from them in tall jets. They walked toward the rear of the building, their progress followed closely by the machine operators.

They passed through another door into a large room that appeared to be an addition to the original building. There they found six men, Travis being the easiest to spot.

Kane shoved Wispy out of the way and stared at the big man, his gun down at his thigh in a non-threatening position. "I hear you're looking for me," Kane said.

"If you're Kane, then that would be true," the man rumbled.

"I'm here to tell you to go home, Bear."

"And if I don't want to?"

"Then you'll be made leave."

"Big man for a loner," one of the other mercenaries stated.

"Hold on," Travis said. "He wouldn't be here if he wasn't sure he could walk back out. How many you got out there?"

"Two teams listening in on everything we're saying," Kane replied.

"We shit two teams for breakfast," another operator said.

"Not these two teams," Kane said.

The man took a threatening step forward, and the gun beside the Team Reaper commander's thigh moved far enough to put a bullet in his leg. The sound echoed through the room as the man collapsed. He grasped at his leg, gritting his teeth in pain. Kane looked at Travis, who seemed on edge, like he was cornered but itching to do something to break out.

"Just calm down, Travis," Kane said. "I have no quarrel with you; otherwise, we'd have come in here, guns blazing and taking no prisoners. This is me giving you a chance. Edison is scum who is using my sister to draw me out. You were his backup plan. I don't want to kill you, but you need to deal yourself out of this one."

"You know we could kill you before your friends get in here, right?"

"I've no doubt," Kane said with a shrug. "But that would be two of us."

"If I agree to go, then we're free to leave?"

"Yes. You'll be under observation by MI5 until you get on the big silver bird, but they'll leave you alone."

"You give me your word?"

Kane nodded.

"All right, we'll go, but if we cross paths again, Kane, things will be different."

"Wouldn't want it any other way."

Travis nodded. "You still looking for Brian Finn?"

Kane was taken aback by the question. "How do you know?"

"Are you or not?"

"Yeah."

"Up near Bainbridge in the north. On the Bain River. There's an estate worth checking out."

"How?"

"Work."

"Thanks."

"Don't thank me. We're even. Next time, one of us will die."

"Can't wait," Kane said with unerring confidence. Then he turned and left.

On his way out the door, he said into his comms, "Did you get that?"

"Copy, Reaper," Thurston acknowledged. "Slick is looking into it as we speak."

"All right, we'll be back soon."

"Roger. Out."

———

"What do you mean, it's off?" Edison hissed.

"Somehow they knew we were here, so the op is over," Travis replied.

"Well, kiss the rest of your payment goodbye."

"It is what it is," he announced. Travis could imagine the varying stages of anger the intelligence boss was going through and thought that he was about to peak.

"You'll never work for this government again, Travis. Do you hear me?"

"Yeah, I hear you, but know this. Kane and his people aren't like anything or anyone you've dealt with before. He'll come for you, and when he does, there'll be no stopping him."

"Let him come," Edison said and hung up.

———

Kane was talking to Thurston, Ferrero, and Fitzgerald from MI5 when Swift brought them the news. He opened the office door with the usual enthusiasm he displayed when he was excited. Thurston shook her head. "Nice of you to knock."

"Yeah, sorry. I found Kyran Finn."

"Where?"

"Stafford on Tythe."

"Where's that?" Kane asked.

"Just outside of London," Fitzgerald replied.

"Is he alone?"

Swift said, "As far as I can tell, it's him, the woman, and the little girl."

"Get me all you can, Slick. I'll be right out."

He disappeared. Ferrero said, "I'll inform the team."

"No," Kane said. "I'll go and take Troy with me."

"Troy's been called back to Global. They've got a job for him. Take Cara."

"Roger that."

"Mr. Kane," Fitzgerald said in a stoic voice. "Kyran Finn is a terrorist and is to be treated as such. He is responsible for the deaths of a lot of people. It would be a shame should he ever have the opportunity to do that again."

"Are you telling me you want me to kill him?" Kane asked.

"It would seem to be the best outcome."

"What about questioning him? Finding out all you can?"

"We know all we need to know. Even the location of his father."

"That's yet to be confirmed," Thurston pointed out.

Fitzgerald ignored her. "Do we have an understanding, Mr. Kane?"

"I understand," Kane answered. "But I'm not going to murder him. If he fights, I'll put him down. If he gives up, I'll bring him in."

"Is that a conscience I detect?" the MI5 man asked cynically.

"Call it whatever you want."

They stared at each other for a long moment like two bull elephants sizing one another up. Fitzgerald nodded. "Do it your way. Just don't let him escape."

"Don't worry, Fitzgerald, he won't escape this time. Not if I have anything to do with it."

Kane left the room and found Cara eating a salad in the kitchen and discussing recipes with Brick. "You actually cook?" Kane asked when he walked in on the conversation.

"I do," Cara replied.

"I wasn't talking to you. I was talking to Doctor Zhivago."

Brick smiled. "I cook the meanest chili you ever tasted."

"There you go. I know Cara can cook; you only have to look at her son."

"Are you saying he's fat?"

"Hell, no. Look how tall he is."

"He gets that from his father," she told them. "What are you doing here, anyway? I thought you had a meeting?"

"We've got a mission. Just you and me. Slick found Kyran Finn."

"What do we know?"

"Let's go find out."

Brick stared at Kane. "You need some help?"

"If we do, I'll call."

"I'll be here."

Cara and Kane went to the ops room and found

Swift at his computer. "What do you have, Slick?" Cara asked, running her hand over his shoulder.

"Ma'am, I've got everything you need."

"Let's have a look."

Swift started with a satellite picture of the place they were looking for. From above, it didn't look like much, but a side-on photo showed a two-floor stone-built house that resembled a box more than anything else. Along its front, close to the narrow road on which it sat, was a stone wall built of the same material as the house.

The driveway went around the back of the house, and the land fell away into a broad gully lined by trees.

"That would be a good approach," Cara said.

"I was thinking that," Kane acknowledged.

"Have we confirmed that they're there?"

"They're there, but we're not sure who else is."

"I guess we'll find out."

———

OUTSIDE STAFFORD ON TYTHE

The night was cold, and a chill wind whistled up the gully, sighing through the trees and masking any noise the two intruders might make. Kane and Cara looked up the slope toward the house. There were lights on, and they'd seen movement inside as a shadow walked past one of the windows.

They took out their Glocks and started up the slope, keeping low in case anyone was watching from inside.

Clouds covered the moon, which made the darkness almost complete. However, they had their NVGs, so the black of the night became the luminescent green they were used to.

When he reached the top of the slope and the stone wall, Kane slid over it, followed immediately by Cara. Kane took his NVGs off and looked through a window. The room was a study or a second living room. It was empty even though the light was on.

Using hand signals, he directed Cara toward the back door, where a glass conservatory protruded from the rear of the house. She tried the door and found it unlocked. With her weapon raised, she slipped inside and walked toward the entrance to the house.

That door was locked.

With Kane covering her, she dropped to a knee and took out her lock picks. "Never leave home without them," she whispered.

Within moments, they were in, the door they'd used shut behind them. The kitchen was brightly lit and had sleek white wall-to-wall cabinets, and an island in the center supported a huge slab of granite. Cara skirted around it and stopped at a door leading into a narrow hall. Across from it was another living room.

The sofa and chairs faced away from the door. Kyran occupied one of the chairs, his attention rigidly fixed on the television. Missy was sprawled on the sofa. There was no sign of the little girl, Kaitlin.

Silently, the pair entered the living room, Kane moving behind Kyran while Cara went for Missy. The younger Finn must have sensed something was wrong because his head whipped around just as Kane was about to place the muzzle of the Glock to it.

"Don't make a sound, Kyran."

The young man's eyes widened. "You."

On the sofa, Missy gasped. Cara said in a calm voice, "Where's the little girl?"

Missy's eyes darted to Kyran.

"Don't look at him," Cara told her. "He's not your friend here; we are. Where's the girl?"

"Don't tell them," Kyran hissed.

Kane clipped him with the Glock hard enough to make his eyes water. "Shut up."

"Where's the girl?" Cara asked once more.

"Upstairs, asleep."

"Go and get her, then bring her back here."

Missy hesitated.

"We're not here to harm you. We're here to keep you safe. We work for MI5."

"Fucking filth," Kyran hissed at Kane. "Dirty lowdown dog."

Kane cocked an eyebrow. "You want me to hit you again? Be thankful you're alive. MI5 wanted me to kill you."

Forcing Kyran onto the floor, Kane zip-tied his hands behind his back.

Missy disappeared from the room, and Cara heard her footsteps on the stairs as she climbed them. She turned to Kane and was about to say something when the power went out.

"That can't be good."

Kane said, "I think we're about to get visitors."

———

Nine men moved like wraiths through the darkness as they climbed out of the same gully Kane and Cara had used on their approach. They were dressed in black and armed with AK-74s. Each wore NVGs but lacked the body armor used by professionals.

As they started up the slope, they split into two teams while the odd man out went for the power box. Once they were in position, a heavily accented Irish voice said, "Do it now."

The lights went out.

————

"They'll come in both doors," Kane said to Cara in an urgent voice as they put their NVGs back on.

"What the fuck is going on?" Kyran wailed.

"Shut the hell up," Cara growled. "I'll take the front, Reaper."

"Roger that," he replied, and as he walked toward the door, he said into his comms. "Zero, this is Reaper One. We're about to have contact with an unknown enemy with unknown numbers, over."

"Copy, Reaper One, will dispatch QRF."

"Roger that."

In the hallway, Cara walked toward the front door. A flashlight beam appeared on the stairs, and Missy's voice said, "What's happening?"

"Get back upstairs and lock yourself in a room."

"What? Why?"

"Do—"

The front door smashed back on its hinges, and Cara heard the high-pitched squeal of the little girl, Kaitlin.

"Get up there, now!" Cara shouted and fired at the first figure that came through the doorway.

The Glock roared three times, and the attacker dropped before he could get over the threshold. Cara heard the sharp reports of Kane's weapon from the kitchen and knew the intruders had breached simultaneously.

Cara threw herself sideways onto the stairs, the narrow alcove shielding her from the heavy burst of automatic fire that ripped down the passage and hammered into the far wall.

She leaned out and fired another couple of shots at the intruders, but they'd ducked out of sight after their comrade had been killed on entry. Cara heard harsh voices as the shooters tried to work out what was happening.

From the kitchen, more shots sounded. Kane had crouched behind the island as he tried to deny the shooters entry. One was down, but the others were unloading their AK magazines at the Team Reaper commander's shelter.

The kitchen was being torn apart. Cabinet doors hung off or came away when bullets hammered into them, turning them into matchsticks. The plates and cups inside shattered, while foodstuffs simply exploded on the shelves.

Kane rose from his refuge and shot a second intruder as he tried to get in. A cry of pain told him his bullets had found their mark.

Then came silence. All firing stopped, and Kane strained to hear sounds that weren't there over the ringing in his ears.

Kane stopped and tried to control his breathing. His heart rate came down, and he closed his eyes. The ringing subsided, and his hearing returned.

The crunch of boot on glass was all the warning he needed.

Kane's eyes flew open, and he came up over the island. Two shooters were trying to sneak through the kitchen door. He fired four times at the man in front. Each round struck home, driving the shooter backward. When he dropped to the floor, it left his friend exposed.

The Reaper went to fire once more, but nothing happened. He'd screwed up. His magazine was empty. "Shit," he growled and dropped behind the island once more.

The shooter opened fire with his AK, shouting at the top of his lungs, hoping he could scare to death the man who'd killed his friends. Kane dropped the empty magazine and replaced it with a fresh one.

Bullets punched into the wall and the island. More debris rained down on the Team Reaper commander as he slammed the new magazine home.

Kane threw himself sideways across the floor and emerged into the open, then raised his weapon and fired three shots. The shooter cried out in pain and fell to the floor, dead.

Lying there and waiting to see if another shooter would appear, Kane was relieved when no one loomed into view. Still, gunfire could be heard from the other end of the house. He said into his comms, "How you doing, Cara?"

"Just grand," she replied. "I'm doing—"

She stopped talking as she shot an intruder dead. "I'm doing just great, Reaper."

"I'm coming your way."

"Watch your ass."

He climbed to his feet and walked toward the hall.

He peered around the corner and saw Cara huddled in the staircase alcove. Bullets from the shooters at the front door tore down the hall and slammed into the wall. He ducked back when a bullet fanned his face.

The shooting suddenly stopped, and everything went quiet. It was an eerie silence pierced only by heavy breathing. Kane called, "Cara, you alright?"

"I'm good."

"What's going on?"

"They've gone."

"Are you sure?"

"Yeah."

Kane came out of cover and walked along the bullet-destroyed hallway. Cara stepped out. "These guys came here with a mission, and it wasn't rescue."

One of the wounded men moaned. Cara bent down to check him. She said, "I can't tell in this light if he'll live or not."

"Let's secure this place and wait for reinforcements. They should be here soon."

"Roger that."

CHAPTER 17

LONDON, ENGLAND

TRAYNOR AND FERRERO entered the interrogation room where Kyran Finn waited. The young man looked up and fixed them with a disdainful look. "How are you doing, Mister Finn?" Ferrero asked. "Are you being looked after?"

Finn looked at the unopened bottle of water in front of him and swept it onto the floor in a childish act of defiance. Ferrero glanced at Traynor. "Make a note that he didn't like the water, Pete. Maybe we can get prisoners Coke from now on."

"I'll let the general know."

They sat down opposite Kyran and stared at him. All three sat in stony silence for what was a ticking-clock-on-the-mantlepiece moment. Ferrero sighed. Six hours had elapsed since the incident at the house outside Stafford on Tythe.

"Kyran, who were those men that came to kill you?"

He stared at the former DEA agent but held his silence.

Ferrero looked at Traynor. "Maybe he needs to see the pictures, Pete."

Traynor placed a folder he'd brought with him on the table and opened it. He spread the pictures it contained across the table. Every pictured man was dead.

"Take a look now, Kyran. I think you might recognize them," Ferrero said.

Kyran ran eyes over the pictures, then stared at Ferrero. "Don't know them."

Traynor raised an eyebrow. "No? You sure?"

"Fuck you."

Traynor stabbed a finger at the first picture. "Colum Byrne, Real IRA."

Nothing.

A second picture. "Doyle Gallagher, New IRA."

Nothing.

More pictures. "Grady Lynch, Provisional IRA. Liam Daly, New IRA. Doran Wilson, Real IRA. Should I go on?"

Silence.

Traynor nodded and grabbed a final picture. "All right, here's the kicker. Braden O'Connor. New IRA and enforcer for Brian Finn. Your father sent these men to kill you, Kyran. You're too much of a loose cannon. A frigging liability."

Kyran stared at the last picture as he tried to work out what was happening. Surely his father wouldn't do this. Not to him. Surely not.

The longer he thought about it, the harder the realization hit him. "That bastard. Rotten gobshite bastard."

"You're awake, then?" Ferrero asked.

"The bastard tried to have me killed."

"To be fair, you did kill the mother of his granddaughter," Traynor pointed out. "And then kidnapped her and Missy."

"She's my daughter."

"You won't be seeing her for a long time. We've got footage of you parking the lorry outside the Mountbatten. You're screwed, mate."

"I want a deal. I'll give you everything you need to know about my father and testify in court."

"Not up to us," Ferrero said.

"Then get someone who can okay it, damn you!"

Traynor put the pictures back in the folder, and he and Ferrero left the room.

They found Thurston and Fitzgerald waiting for them in the hall. "Are you willing to do it?" Ferrero asked the MI5 man.

"Depends on what he gives us," Fitzgerald allowed. "I can have the paperwork done up and sent over. It doesn't help that he hasn't actually asked for anything."

Traynor said, "I think he'll take anything with a light at the end of the tunnel."

Fitzgerald sighed. "All right. Give me an hour, and I'll see what I can come up with."

———

They reentered the interrogation room seventy minutes later. Ferrero held a piece of paper in his hand. "I've got what you want right here, Kyran."

"How do you know what I want?" the younger Finn sneered.

"Let me tell you," Ferrero replied. "You will give us what you know about your father and his operation and testify in court, and in return, you will be given a maximum term of incarceration of thirty-five years."

"What?" Kyran exploded.

"Take it or leave it, Kyran. However, hear this. If you don't take it, you'll die in prison. This way, you'll have a chance of getting out. Plus, your father will be put away as well. You want him out there free after he tried to kill you?"

"Not good enough. I want less time."

"No."

"Then good luck."

Ferrero and Traynor stood up. "Then good luck with MI5."

They turned and started toward the door.

"Wait."

"Got something to say?" Traynor asked.

The anxiety was evident on Kyran's face. "I want my daughter to go to my sister. Keira has nothing to do with my da's business."

Ferrero nodded. "I think we can do that."

"Then I'll tell you whatever you want to know."

They sat back down.

"Let's start with the bridge bombings. How did they get into the country?" Ferrero asked.

"We got them in on a ship."

"By we, you mean you and your father?"

"Da gave it the tick of approval, and I did the rest." Finn looked down at his hands and began picking his fingernails.

"So, he did nothing?" Ferrero was disappointed by the revelation.

"He just oversaw it."

"What about the materials they used?"

"I got them."

"The lorries?" Traynor's voice was hopeful.

"Me again."

Ferrero was starting to worry about the way the questioning was going. So far, Brian Finn hadn't really done anything. "Hasan Kubar. How is it you know him?"

"My da knows him from the old days."

"What do you mean, the old days?"

"Back when the PIRA was allied with Libya."

"So he reached out to your father to get him into the country?"

"Yes."

"And your father organized it?"

"No. I did."

Ferrero paused, then, "Tell me about the Exchange bombing."

"What do you want to know?"

"Whose idea was it?"

"Da's."

"He organized it?"

"No, he left that to me."

Did Finn do anything?

"You got the lorry for it?"

"Yes."

"Why bomb the Exchange?" Traynor asked.

"It was to make a statement against what the politicians were trying to do to our country," Kyran explained.

"They were trying to unite it," Ferrero said.

"Yes, but they were giving control to the British."

"Only for a few years until Ireland was back on her feet."

"That's what they say," Kyran snarled. "But give them an inch, and the gobshites will take a frigging mile."

"What happened to Murphy?" Ferrero asked.

"Braden killed him."

"Why?"

Kyran remained silent.

"If you want the deal, Kyran, you need to answer the questions," Ferrero pointed out.

"I ordered him to do it because I didn't trust Murphy."

"Why?"

The younger Finn shrugged. "I didn't trust him."

"How did your father take it?"

"He wasn't happy."

"The Fairfield siege?"

"Da told me what he wanted, and I did the rest."

"You organized it?"

"Yes."

"What was the idea behind it?"

"To make a statement."

"Did the ones in the Estate siege know it was going to be a one-way trip?"

"The ones that mattered."

Cold.

"Where's your father?" Ferrero asked.

"Place up north on a river outside of a town called Bainbridge."

At least he wasn't lying. Ferrero gave him the piece of paper and a pen. "Sign that."

Once Kyran was finished, he put the pen on the paper. "Now what?"

"MI5 will take you and ask you more questions."

Kyran nodded. "Can I see my daughter before I go?"

Traynor shook his head. "Not going to happen."

"Why not?"

"You figure it out."

They left the room and found Hank Jones with Thurston and Fitzgerald. Ferrero looked at the MI5 man. "He's all yours."

"My people will get whatever they need from him."

Jones said, "Well done. Now all you need to do is roll up the rest of the snake."

"Reaper and the team will take care of that. However, what worries me is that Finn had his son do most of the heavy lifting. A good lawyer will say he was acting on his own."

"Maybe you'll get lucky, and he'll resist," Fitzgerald said.

"Don't count on it," Ferrero replied. "I think he's had it planned this way right from the get-go."

"Then why have his man kill Kyran if he was using him that way?"

"Because the kid was too unstable. Without the kid, he knew there'd be trouble linking him to it all."

"Have Arenas and Kane draw up a plan immediately, Luis," Thurston said. "I want them ready to go tonight."

"Can't do that, ma'am," Swift said, interrupting. "Finn is leaving the country in four hours."

"Where's he going?"

"Iran."

"Why would he be going there?"

"I tracked a boatload of money being funneled into one of Finn's shell companies that came through all these different channels and originated from another shell company that is run by the Iranian government."

"What you're saying is that Iran sponsored the bombing?"

"Yes, ma'am."

"Right," Ferrero growled. "That little prick lied."

He turned and stormed back toward the doorway. Thurston called after him, "Don't kill him, Luis."

"Not yet, Mary. Not frigging yet."

Traynor said, "I'd better—"

Thurston nodded. "Yes, it might be best."

————

Ferrero slammed Kyran's head down on the hard table and held it there. He lowered his own head so his mouth was close to the younger Finn's ear. "You little fuck, you didn't tell me everything."

Traynor came in behind them and moved to one side, close enough to intervene if he had to.

"What are you doing, you bloody lunatic?" Kyran wailed.

Ferrero lifted the man's head a fraction and slammed it down again. "The Iranians. You didn't mention them."

"You didn't ask."

"And you conveniently forgot to mention them."

Another whack on the table and Ferrero let him go. "Speak, or by Christ, I'll take that offer off the table and throw you into the darkest hole I can find."

"Da was about broke. His businesses were in decline—"

"You mean his criminal enterprises."

"Yes. He was approached by someone from the Iranian consulate with a proposition. Help the Libyans get into the country, and they'd pay him for it."

It made sense, Iranians sponsoring terror organizations.

"How much?"

"Twenty million."

"So, he used some of that money to bankroll his own attack on London," Ferrero theorized.

"Yes. Only he didn't know about the meeting at the time. It wasn't until he found out that he asked me to put the operation together."

"Why didn't he do it himself?"

"I don't know. I guess he wanted me to prove myself," Kyran answered.

"You're just a dumb shithead, aren't you? Your father didn't want you to prove yourself. He was covering his own ass in case it went south."

Ferrero let that sink in for a few moments.

"Who was the Iranian?"

"What?"

"The Iranian that reached out to your father. Who was he?"

"Aram Shirvani."

"Is there anything else?"

"No."

Ferrero glared at him. "You'd better pray there isn't."

————

"Who is Aram Shirvani?" Ferrero asked Fitzgerald.

"An Iranian diplomat we suspect is coordinating terrorist strikes throughout Europe. Why?"

"He met with Brian Finn and offered him money to get the terrorist cell into the country. Finn was strapped, so he agreed to it. He then used some of the twenty million he was paid to fund his own act of terror after finding out about the meeting."

"Shirvani is always in town when something goes bang. I can make a call to see if he's still in London or was."

"Don't you know?"

"I've been a bit busy lately."

"Make the call. I've got a team to get ready."

Jones said, "Tell Reaper I want to see him."

"Just as soon as I find him, Hank," Ferrero replied.

The former DEA man left them to their talk while he went to find the team. When he did, he said to Kane, "Hank Jones is here and wants to see you."

"What about?"

"No idea." He turned to Cara. "While Kane is talking to Jones, I want you to start getting ready to be deployed. You've got an hour to get it done."

"Yes, sir."

———

"Reaper."

"General."

"How's it going, son?"

"All right, I guess," Kane replied, unsure of where the conversation was going.

"Have you given much thought to your sister?"

"As soon as we're done here, we're going after her."

"I thought you would," Jones acknowledged. "Listen, let me know when the time comes, and I'll direct some Global assets your way. I've been talking to Alex Joseph, and he's monitoring the situation from his end. Hunt and Rucker are his boots on the ground."

"Thank you, sir."

"Have you given any thought to how you're going to get into the country?" Jones asked.

"Carlos says he can get us in through Mexico."

"I'll have a talk with him. I've got some friends who owe me a favor, and they'll be able to get your team farther north from the border."

"Any help would be appreciated, sir. But I'd rather use the admiral."

Jones nodded. "All right, Reaper. You've got a mission to plan. Good luck."

"Thank you, sir."

CHAPTER 18

BAIN RIVER, NEAR BAINBRIDGE

"ALL CALLSIGNS HOLD," Cara said in a hushed voice over the team's comms.

"What is it, Reaper Two?" Kane asked.

"I've got a rover on the estate perimeter," she replied.

"Is he the only one?" Kane asked.

"The only one I can see so far."

"Take him out."

The suppressed L129 centered on the sentry and followed his track. Cara let out a long breath and squeezed the trigger.

She felt the comfort of the weapon slamming back against her shoulder as she watched the armed man drop in his tracks. "Tango down."

Cara moved farther along the river to a point where she could change course and climb the bank to the perimeter fence made of stone. Once she made it, she waited for the others. The first to reach her was Brick, followed by Axe, then Kane, and finally Knocker.

Kane looked at her. "You wait here and cover us as we go in."

"Roger that."

Tapping Brick on the shoulder, Kane said, "You're up."

"Roger that."

The former SEAL cleared the fence and started across the open ground between the rest of the team and a two-story house with a thatched roof. As soon as he'd gone five meters, Knocker followed him, then Axe, and finally Kane.

Cara said into her comms, "Bravo One, what's the sitrep on the rovers, over?"

"So far, so good...wait one."

Cara took a deep breath, then Reynolds came back. "Reaper Two, the east side of the house."

Cara moved her scope and saw the sentry appear. He was armed with an AK-74. She settled her sights on the shooter and squeezed the trigger. The man jerked and fell to the gray pavers he'd been walking along. "Got him, Bravo One."

Moving her eye away from the sights, Cara checked on the progress of the others. They still had a ways to go. She started sweeping the mullioned windows of the house, stopping when she saw movement on the second floor, top right.

"Reaper, we've got movement at the top right window."

"Deal with it. We're sitting ducks out here."

Cara waited, the scope and rifle unwavering. She recognized the figure in the window as a man when he froze long enough for her to get a clear look at him. He reached out and opened the window, and that was enough. Cara shot him in the chest.

"Reaper, the tango is down, but you need to step it up a little."

"Roger that."

From her position, she saw the rest of the team pick up their pace. They hit the paved area at the rear of the house at a run and burst into the kitchen through the rear door. Then the firing started.

———

Axe shot the first person he saw with a weapon. The problem was the shooter squeezed the trigger as he was dying and sprayed the kitchen with half a magazine of bullets from his AK-74. If the rest of the house hadn't already been warned, they were now.

"Good one, cock," Knocker said to him as he walked past. "Just blow a frigging bugle next time."

"Kiss my ass."

Another shooter appeared in the door that led into the kitchen. Knocker shot him and pressed forward. "Fucking cowboy."

The Brit led them through the house, Kane bringing up the rear. He heard Knocker shout, "Stop right there, you skiving bog-trotter."

When Kane caught up with them, Brian Finn was on his knees, and his hands were being zip-tied behind his back. Brick had Keira off to one side and was doing the same to her. When she saw him, her eyes widened. "You? I don't understand."

"My name is John Kane. I work for the Global

Corporation. We're seconded to the British government and MI5."

"You were a bloody plant?" Finn asked incredulously.

"Something like that."

"The rest of the house is clear, Reaper," Axe said.

"Come on in, Cara," Kane said into his comms.

"What...what about the man you shot? You killed?" Keira asked.

"That was me," Knocker said with a large grin. "I got bit by a cobra in Libya too, but it was a dry bite. Thought I was screwed for a moment."

"It was you at the Projects and then at Stafford on Tythe." It was a statement.

Kane looked at Finn and nodded. "We also know about the Iranians. We know everything and how you were behind it all."

"What Iranians?" Keira asked.

Cara appeared in the doorway. Kane motioned to Keira. "Cut her loose, Cara."

While she did that, Kane answered her question. "The Iranians came to your father to get the Libyan terrorists into the country. Offered him twenty million to do it. So, he got your brother to organize it all."

She looked at her father. "Is this true?"

"No."

"He had your brother do everything so he would remain clean. Then, when it looked like it was all falling apart, he tried to have your brother killed."

Keira's face fell. "I-I knew about that."

Kane stared at her. "He wants you to take care of the little girl. But now, I don't know."

"What do you mean?"

"You just admitted to knowing about the attempt to kill your brother. That makes you an accessory."

"Don't be foolish. Do you think I could have stopped it?"

"Not my decision to make."

"She had nothing to do with it," Finn snarled. "It was all my doing."

Kane looked at Cara. "Well, at least we have him on something."

She nodded. "It's a start."

Kane pressed his transmit button. "Zero, this is Reaper One. Target is secure and HVT in custody."

"Roger that, Reaper One. Good job."

———

LONDON, ENGLAND

"That's that, then," Thurston said with a long sigh.

Fitzgerald nodded. "It's been great working with you and your people. I'll call again, I'm sure."

"What about Aram Shirvani?"

"If he was in the country as suggested, he's gone now. I've handed it off to my counterpart at MI6. I'm sure they will know what to do with the information." He paused. "What now for your people?"

"We've got to go home. Unfinished business."

"Kane's sister?"

"Yes. We need to get her out."

"If there's anything you need, just ask."

"I will."

The MI5 man left, and Thurston went to find the

others. "Everyone, pack up. We're headed back to Hereford."

"What about Reaper's sister, ma'am?" Axe asked.

"Once we get to Hereford, we'll work out a plan. But don't worry; she's our next mission."

"Yes, ma'am."

They started to go about their business, but Ferrero pulled Thurston to one side. "Mary, I'm having doubts about going back to the US."

"Me too," she allowed.

"We're risking the whole team for one person," Ferrero pointed out.

"Are you going to be the one to try to stop them?"

He shook his head. "I suggest we send Kane and no one else."

"You're saying we send him on his own, is that right?"

"That's exactly what I'm saying."

"They're not going to like it."

"The team is bigger than one man. Besides, I'm sure he'll get all the help he needs once he gets there."

Thurston knew he was right. "All right, Luis. We'll break it to them when we get to Hereford."

"Yes, ma'am."

———

HEREFORD, ENGLAND

The two commanders gathered their people into the briefing room. Since it had been Ferrero's idea, he was the one who broke the news to the rest of the team. "There's no easy way to say this so, I'm just going to put it out there. You can all then have your say, and that will be the end of it. Reaper will be the only one going to the States after his sister."

As predicted, the uproar came from everyone except Kane.

"What bullshit is this?" Axe asked. "He can't go there on his own."

"It's a load of fucking bollocks if you ask me," Knocker said.

"I know you don't like it—" Ferrero started.

"It sucks," Reynolds growled.

"But after a discussion, we've decided we can't risk all of the team just for one person."

"We've done it before," Brick pointed out.

"I agree. But this time, they know someone is coming."

"He's right," Kane said. "They're expecting us, but one person might be able to get in under the radar."

"That's crazy, Reaper," Cara said. "If Edison catches you, he won't give you a trial. He'll kill you. Remember, he's selling guns to whoever wants them, and he knows we know."

"I'll be fine. Carlos, you still got that friend who'll get me into the country?"

"On speed dial, *amigo*."

"Don't suppose you know where I can get a ride, General?"

"I'm sure we can organize something, Reaper."

"Appreciate it."

"I still don't like this, Reaper," Cara said.

Kane smiled thinly. "It is what it is."

After the meeting broke up, she followed him out of the room. "Take me with you, Reaper."

He stared at her long and hard, considering it before shaking his head. "I can't. What about Jimmy? If something happened to you, he'd have no one."

"Do you always have to be right?" she snapped.

He wrapped his arms around her. "I'll be back. I promise."

————

RAF BRIZE NORTON, OXFORDSHIRE, ENGLAND

Kane threw his duffel under the seat in the cargo bay of the C-17 and sat down. He looked at the loadmaster and asked, "How soon before we're wheels up?"

"We're waiting on some more cargo, mate. Shouldn't be too long."

Kane nodded and sat down. He stretched his legs out and laid his head back against the fuselage. He sat like that for a few minutes, then he sensed something occurring around him. He opened his eyes and turned his head to look at the top of the ramp. He was surprised to see four people standing there.

Cara, Knocker, Brick, and Axe. All had duffel bags and steely looks of determination on their faces.

"What are you doing here?" Kane asked.

"The general gave us a few days off," Cara replied. "Said, we deserved it. We all decided to take an overseas holiday."

"You'll never guess where to." Axe grinned.

"The Bahamas?" Kane asked sarcastically.

"If you're going to be like that, I'm not going to tell you."

"It rhymes with Mexico," Knocker said.

"Dipshit, you went and told him," Axe growled.

"Told him what?"

"That we were going to Mexico."

"Oh, that."

"You two done?" Kane asked.

They both shrugged. "Pretty much."

Kane looked at them and knew there was no use arguing. "Well, you might as well get seated so we can take off."

Cara smiled. "In a moment. We've got some equipment that needs loading first."

CHAPTER 19

UNITED STATES/MEXICO BORDER

IT WAS AN OLD TUNNEL, mostly used by coyotes for traversing the border with drugs and getting illegals across. Right now, it was being utilized by five armed Americans and one Mexican who wore a Yankees baseball cap and seemed edgy. Maybe a little too edgy.

After the team touched down in Mexico City, they had been taken to a location in a small town where they could organize themselves. From there, they were driven north to a remote location on the Arizona border where the tunnel was located. Sure, there were other tunnels they could have used, but this one was their best option. Or so Manuel had insisted.

"How much farther, Manuel?" Kane asked.

"Not long now, *amigo*," he said nervously.

Kane broke squelch on his comms three times to warn the others that something wasn't right. They answered him by doing it once in reply.

The whole tunnel was lit. At the Mexican end, a

large, camouflaged generator provided the power required to light the three-quarter-mile-long passage.

Five minutes later, they reached the US end. Manuel turned to Kane. "Wait here. I will check to see that the way is clear."

The Mexican disappeared, and Kane turned to his team. He flicked his M6 off safe and said, "I don't like this. Something's off."

"Roger that," Brick said in a low voice.

Manuel returned after a few minutes. "It is clear."

Kane looked at his watch. It was 03:00, and they still had around ten klicks to go to rendezvous with their pickup. Supposedly.

Knocker stepped forward, "I'll take point with Manuel."

"What is the matter, *amigo*?" Manuel asked.

The Brit looked at him. "You make me nervous."

"I what?"

"Something isn't right, and if I walk out there into a trap, then I'm going to take you down with me."

The Mexican started to sweat. "What do you mean?"

"Just get out there," Knocker growled, giving him a shove.

"No, wait. I—"

"There it is," the Brit said. "I think we're going to need our NVGs."

"Who's out there?" Kane asked.

"N-no one."

"Try again."

"I-I..."

Axe took out his Glock and placed it under the frightened man's chin. "I didn't quite catch that."

"Jose Ramirez."

"Who is Jose Ramirez?"

"He is the coyote who owns this tunnel."

"What does he want with us?"

"More to the point," Cara asked., "why is he on US soil?"

"He is working with the one called El Oso."

"Well, fuck me," Brick growled. "Bear Travis."

"*Sí*, that is him."

"How many men?" Kane asked.

"Maybe ten."

"Where are they?"

"Lining the arroyo outside."

Kane looked at Cara. "Looks like you were right to have a backup plan."

She nodded. "Reaper Two to Scimitar, over."

"Good to hear your voice, Reaper Two."

"We seem to have a situation on the home side."

"Roger that. Give us a couple of minutes, and we'll take care of it for you."

"Copy, Scimitar. Be aware that the bad guys number ten."

"That's ten, Reaper Two. Confirm?"

"Affirmative."

"Roger that. Snake Team is inbound."

"What...what is going on?" Manuel asked.

"We've organized a little surprise for our surprise."

———

The DPVs, or Desert Patrol Vehicles, came out of the darkness. Their growl foretold their coming, but when they appeared, Bear Travis was still found wanting.

The deep chug-chug of the fifty-caliber weapons on the vehicles boomed through the darkness, tracer rounds visible by the laser-like trail they left behind them. Shouts of alarm came as the wicked heavy-caliber bullets found targets in the night.

Hunt spun the wheel and planted his foot on the gas pedal. Standing and operating the fifty was Rucker, who swept the landscape, looking for more targets.

It didn't last long. The ambushers scattered to the four winds when they realized how much trouble they were in. They melted back into the darkness and disappeared.

"Reaper," Hunt said into his comms, "you can come on out. They're gone."

Kane and the others emerged from the tunnel on the American side. Hunt and he shook hands. "Good to see you, Bord."

"You, too."

"What's the damage?"

"We got a few of them. I'm just waiting for a final tally."

There was silence for a moment before Kane asked, "How is she?"

"From what I gather through different channels, she's doing all right. Alex tried to get in to see her, but Edison wouldn't let him."

"Asshole."

"He is that. Ever since you pulled that television stunt, the admiral has been looking into the son of a bitch on the downlow. Looks like you all were right. He's been selling weapons to whoever wants to pay for them. Before that, while the Cabal was active, he was hip-deep in it with them."

"So, this is all about revenge," Kane theorized.

"Pretty much."

"Where does he have her?"

"There's a facility in Virginia near Elkton. Just outside Shenandoah National Park. *Officially*, it's a veterans' repatriation hospital. What it is, is a secure facility utilized by the NIS for all their dirty secrets."

"What's their security like?"

"Pretty tight. You'll have to go in hot."

Kane wasn't too happy about that. "Is there another way?"

"You could always scoop Edison up and use him as a hostage."

"It might come to that. But first, we need to get as far away from here as possible before every government agency with a letter in its name is crawling up our asses."

"Might be an idea."

WASHINGTON, DC

Edison looked at the screen, his face a mask of concern. "What fucking happened?"

"We got our asses handed to us," Travis said. "We were lucky to get out alive."

"That's twice, Travis. I don't like paying for failure."

"I'll deliver what I said I would," Bear growled.

"Make sure you do. Christ, do I have to do it all myself?"

"Maybe you should."

"Whatever. Get it done."

The connection was lost, and Edison sat in the chair behind the desk and brooded about the fact that Kane and his team had been able to come onto US soil. Now they were out there, and he had no idea where.

As he stared out through the walls of his glass cubicle, his expression changed. Approaching the door was the only man in the world he was wary of—apart from John Kane, that was.

The gray-haired Alex Joseph opened the door and stormed in.

"Don't bother knocking. Come on in."

"What the hell do you think you're up to, Edison?" Joseph growled.

"I don't know what you mean?"

"No? You hired a bounty hunter as well as a wanted people-smuggler to do your dirty work. Plus, you buy and sell arms to anyone who wants to buy them. You're fucking screwed, Edison."

"Why don't you just go back to sea, Joseph, and get the—" He stopped and thought for a moment. "It was you."

"Damn right, it was me," the former admiral snarled.

"You interfered with the apprehension of wanted fugitives of the United States government. When the President hears about this, you're done."

"Go right ahead, asshole. I'm sure he would like to see the file I have on you."

"You've got nothing."

"Keep it up, and we'll see."

"Get out."

Joseph turned and started toward the door.

Suddenly he stopped and looked back at Edison. "Oh, yeah...have a nice fucking day."

Edison, an angry scowl on his face, watched him leave. Once the former admiral was gone, he took out his encrypted cell, dialed a number, and said, "I've got a job for you."

———

"Someone's following us," the driver said over his shoulder as the black SUV bounced through an intersection.

"I knew the son of a bitch couldn't help himself."

The man in the passenger seat had seen the tail as well. "Blue GMC. I think there might be a second back there too."

"Got it," said the driver. "Another blue GMC."

Both driver and passenger wore combat gear. The passenger reached for his comms and pressed the transmit button. "Falcon Two, this is Falcon One, copy? Over."

"Read you Lima Charlie, Falcon One, over."

"Anvil, we've picked up two tails. Blue GMCs."

"I've got them, Striker," Anvil replied.

"Are we just going to let these assholes tail us?" former Senior Chief Grady Ruggles[1] asked in his familiar gruff voice. "Or are we going to run those motherfuckers off the road and give them a dirt nap?"

Every man in the escort CIA Director Alex Joseph had with him were former SEALs. Now they were part of his revamped Special Projects Unit, along with Hunt and Rucker.

"Patience, Chief," Striker said. "We'll say hello eventually."

"Why fuck around with them, Striker? Just hit them hard and bust a cap in their pussy asses."

Striker chuckled. "You've got to be shitting me."

"You got a problem with me, Squid?" Ruggles growled.

"Yeah, you sound like a frigging teenager from the eighties. 'Bust a cap in their asses.'"

"Maybe I grew up in the right era. Ever thought of that?"

"It's all I ever heard through BUDs. Big hair, big pants, and big dicks."

"And don't you forget it."

"Make a right here."

Ruggles turned right at the next intersection and drove down a side street. The two GMCs followed. "They still back there, Striker?" Joseph asked.

"Yes, sir. You must have been on your best behavior, huh?"

"I might have been a little short with him."

Ruggles grinned. "You tore him a new one, didn't you?"

"Asshole needed it."

"Which means you wanted him to react."

"Maybe."

"Well, you got your wish, Admiral. Now just leave it up to us door-kickers, and we'll do the rest."

Ruggles turned left into a vacant alley without being told to. Striker looked at his former instructor and asked, "What are you doing?"

"What I'm paid to do."

"Shit. Anvil, close up. The chief has just gone off the reservation. Weapons hot."

Ruggles stomped on the brakes, flipped off his belt, and flung the door open, grabbing for his Heckler and Koch 416 as he climbed out.

Striker said as he flung his own door open, "Keep your head down, Admiral."

By the time his boots touched the pavement, Ruggles was shouting, "Get out of the vehicle, mother-fucker, *now*!"

Striker slipped down the other side of their SUV, his weapon at his shoulder and the red-dot sight centered on the windshield of the first GMC.

All four doors on the vehicle came open and armed men came out of them. The first opened fire at the former senior chief, but he was too quick on the trigger. His bullets flew wide, but the former SEAL chief made no such mistake. His first fusillade of gunfire dropped the shooter beside the GMC.

Striker joined the battle and killed a second shooter.

Anvil and his team pulled up behind the second GMC, boxing in the two SUVs. Three men climbed out of the vehicle and joined the battle. The trapped men from the GMCs didn't stand a chance.

Before long, most of them were down. Only two of the eight were still alive, and both were wounded—one in the arm, the other in the leg.

Joseph approached them with a grim expression on his face. "Who are you?"

They remained silent.

Ruggles gave the closest one to him a love tap with the butt of his weapon. "Answer the man."

"Trent," the man growled.

"And you?" the CIA boss asked the second of the wounded.

"Peters."

"Who do you work for?"

Their expressions changed, and they went silent again.

Joseph held out his right hand. "Senior Chief."

Ruggles took the M17 from his leg holster and passed it to the former admiral. Joseph placed the muzzle against Peters' forehead. "Son, one thing my boys know about me is that I don't fuck around. I'll give you one chance, and only one. All I want to know is who you work for."

"Just tell him, Pete," Trent said.

"We work for the NSA, doing odd jobs."

"Who sent you after me?"

"I don't know. Jakes would be the guy to ask. He was our team leader, but he's dead."

Joseph lowered the gun to his side. "You boys want to come and work for the CIA?"

Peters looked surprised. "What?"

"Rather have you working for me than have to kill you later. The choice is yours."

They looked at each other, then agreed to Joseph's terms.

"Fine. Anvil will see that you get the attention you need. Welcome to the CIA."

Striker, Ruggles, and Joseph climbed back into their SUV, and Striker turned in his seat to face his boss. "Are you sure that's the right decision?"

"I guess we'll find out. If it's not, I expect you to deal with it."

"Yes, sir."

"Good. Now let's go back to Langley and see if I can screw that prick's day up a little more."

———

The last person Edison expected to see walk toward his glass cubicle was President Richard Nelson, escorted by his Secret Service detail. The intelligence commander came to his feet as Nelson entered the room and waved at his escort to stay outside.

"I'm surprised to see you here, sir. Did I miss a memo about a meeting?"

"I wouldn't have to be here if you'd kept me up to date on everything that was going on," Nelson hissed, his dark eyes glaring at Edison in anger.

"Sir?"

"Why am I only learning about the border fiasco from Homeland and not you? It's as bad as learning the other shit from the fucking BBC. I'm still cleaning that up."

"Homeland?"

"That's what I said. What happened?"

"Alex Joseph."

"That old fool?"

"He's not much of a fool. Not only did he take out a team of Bear Travis' best men, but also a team from the NSA that was sent to detain him yesterday."

"Christ." Nelson sat down. "So now Kane and his team, whom we worked hard to get rid of under your advice, are loose on United States soil."

"Yes, sir."

"Why?"

"Sir?"

"They were gone. Why are they back?"

"He might be here after his sister, sir."

"But she's in a coma."

"Maybe not," Edison replied.

"What do you mean?"

"His sister is awake and recovering in a facility I had her moved to in Virginia."

Nelson's face darkened. "And you were going to tell me this when?"

"I thought it best not to."

"I'm beginning to think you better catch me up. Start from the beginning."

It took ten minutes of back and forth to get the whole story out. Once it was, Nelson's dark mood was even darker. "Why couldn't you just leave it alone? We were rid of them."

"While they are still around, we'll never be rid of them. All they have to do is dig deep enough, and they'll find that the money being funneled into your campaign is coming from arms sales being made on the side of weapons from war zones in the Middle East that were supposed to have been destroyed."

"Might I remind you that it was your idea?" Nelson growled.

"It doesn't matter whose idea it was. The public and the Justice Department won't give a shit. The only way to stop it from getting out is to take them off the board."

"What do you propose?"

"In times like these, the best ally any government can have is the public. I say we put a bounty on Kane and see what happens."

"How much are we talking?"

"Ten million. Most people I know would kill their own mother for that amount."

"You're talking dead or alive?"

"Exactly."

"Let me think about it."

"What about Joseph?"

"Leave him for the time being. The guy is surrounded by a virtual army. The only way to get rid of him is to remove him, and the guy is a frigging hero in the eyes of the people. The only way to do it is after the coming election. So, no more sending your goons to do wet work."

"Yes, sir."

———————

HEREFORD, ENGLAND

"Any news?" Thurston asked Ferrero.

"Kane checked in a while ago. They've had no more trouble since the border incident."

"You look troubled," she pointed out.

"It's this whole thing."

"No, I know you, Luis. There's something more specific."

"I've got Slick digging into the money side of things with Edison, and as you know, it mostly comes back to arms dealing and such. However, there are a lot of shell companies involved, which the funds pass through."

"That's to be expected."

Ferrero nodded. "Slick traced the weapons back to their source. That was easy because Edison wasn't really worried about that part, only where the money is going."

"Where did the weapons come from?"

"Every Middle East war zone America has been involved in in the past five years. Yemen, Libya, Somalia, Nigeria, Afghanistan, Syria. Even ISIS weapons that were taken from the battlefield. All are contracted to be disposed of by an international company called Triton Arms Disposal."

"I think I've heard of them," Thurston said.

"They are a subsidiary of Hinton Holdings. Hinton Holdings is owned by a conglomeration of people, not the least of whom is President Richard Nelson."

Thurston was stunned. "How could that be?"

"It's never a problem until someone finds out."

"So, he's involved too?"

Ferrero shrugged. "Just because he is in on it doesn't mean he's actually part of it. However, if he is, the BBC report will have shaken him up a bit."

"Great, that's all the people need. One crooked President was replaced by another. And with an election coming up."

"No one knew Carter was who he was," Ferrero pointed out. "Only a select few. Now, we know that Edison isn't Cabal anymore, which is a good thing. But..."

"We're still up against one of the most powerful entities in the modern world. When will it end?"

"Not any time soon," Swift said as he approached them.

Thurston closed her eyes. "Don't tell me, more bad news."

"I found out where the money was going," the

computer tech informed them. "To Nelson's presidential campaign."

"That's it. This is too much. Give Alex Joseph what you've found and pull them out now."

"Kane isn't going to come home now he's there."

"Just try. Even if he doesn't, the rest have to. Get them out."

"I'll do my best."

---

1. Striker, Anvil, and Ruggles made their first appearance in *The Death Bringers*

CHAPTER 20

VIRGINIA, UNITED STATES

"SAY AGAIN, ZERO?" Kane asked, thinking he had not heard it right.

"You're all to pull out immediately, Reaper," Ferrero stated once again. "The situation is such that you are all in danger of—"

"I'm not going anywhere, Luis," Kane cut him off.

"I thought that's what you'd say. The decision is up to you. However, the rest of the team is to get out now. New information has come to light which is very worrying. Do you understand?"

"What if they don't want to go?"

"You make them go, Reaper. You get them on transport back here as soon as possible."

"I'll do what I can, Luis."

"I'll expect to hear they are on their way in the next hour."

The channel went silent, and Kane looked at the

large log cabin where they all were staying. It was a CIA safe house provided by Alex Joseph.

He turned when he heard three vehicles approach, his hand dropping to the holster on his thigh. The SUVs pulled up, and Kane watched as armed operators climbed out. One of them moved to the rear door of the second vehicle and opened it.

Kane recognized a few of them. However, the passenger was unmistakable. "Howdy, Admiral."

"Gunny. You talk to that boss of yours yet?"

"I should have known you wouldn't be out here for the mountain air."

"They thought I could use my influence."

Kane looked at the others. "Striker. Senior Chief."

"Reaper."

"Reaper."

"The muscle for me?" Kane asked.

Joseph shook his head. "No. Mary said if you want to stay, we can help you. The others are expected on a plane in two hours."

"Hey, Reaper, what's going on?" Knocker called from the porch of the log cabin.

Kane looked at the Brit. "Get everyone together, Knocker. The plan's changed."

———

"The hell you say," Axe growled upon hearing the news.

"What's changed?" Cara asked.

Kane shrugged. "I don't know."

Joseph cleared his throat. "I think I might be able to enlighten you some."

"Have at it, Admiral."

"Edison is dealing illegal weapons; you already know that. However, the money from that venture is being funneled into President Nelson's campaign fund. We think that is why you've been targeted. If you got wind of what was going on, it would come out. Now that they know you're here, every agency in the land is going to be looking for you."

"What about you?"

Joseph shook his head. "No. They already tried to kill me. I don't think they'll try again in a hurry."

"So, we're supposed to pack up and head back."

"That's about it," Kane said.

"What about Melanie?" Cara asked.

"The admiral will keep an eye on her," he lied.

Joseph glanced sideways at him but remained silent.

Kane said, "You've got fifteen mikes to get everything together."

They dispersed to get their gear. Kane walked over to Joseph. "I need a ride to get me there."

The CIA director nodded. "Striker, Senior Chief. Give the man a ride."

"Aye, sir."

Striker said, "We'd better get going if we're leaving before the others are done."

"Wait a moment," Joseph said, and reached into his pocket.

After a few minutes, the CIA director said, "That's about it, son. You good to go?"

"I'm ready," Kane replied. He stared at Joseph.

The CIA director nodded. "I'll tell them, son. Good luck."

The men were gone before the others came out with their gear. Cara looked around. "Where is he?"

"Where's who?"

"Don't shit me, Admiral," Cara growled.

Joseph sighed. "He's gone."

"And you let him go? Just like that? With no help?"

"Not exactly. I sent Striker and Ruggles with him."

"You've got to be—"

"What's going on?" Knocker asked as the others walked into the room.

"The admiral let Reaper go off on his own."

"What kind of dodgy wanker are you?" Knocker seethed.

Joseph's eyes narrowed. "Stand down, son. You are all under orders to be evacuated from the continent and sent home to England. I aim to see those orders fulfilled if I have to kick all your asses to do it." He glared at Cara. "That goes for you too, missy."

For a moment, it appeared as though they were about to close on Joseph. Then Cara said, "Stand down."

Joseph nodded. "Right. We're out of here in a couple of minutes. Be ready to go."

———

OUTSIDE OF ELKTON, VIRGINIA

"What do you want us to do, Reaper?" Striker asked Kane as he geared up. They had supplied him with a suppressed Heckler and Koch 416 carbine, a P226 handgun, night-vision goggles, body armor, and ammunition.

Kane turned to them. "A diversion would be good."

"I'm sure we can give you a small one."

"Small one be fucked," Ruggles told him. "You'll get the biggest screw-you diversion since the desert in ninety-one."

Kane smiled in the darkness. Striker said, "You've got it."

"How do you figure on getting out of there, Gunny?" Ruggles asked.

"I'll figure something out. Give me thirty minutes, then make some noise."

"Good luck, Reaper," Striker said.

"Yeah," added Ruggles. "Kick that bastard's ass."

Kane disappeared into the darkness of the surrounding trees. The fluorescence of the NVGs lit the way through the forest to the perimeter fence. He reached into his pocket and took out a set of wire cutters. Within a few moments, he had a large enough hole in the fence to slip through.

But he waited.

For a full five minutes he waited, then two more, after which two figures appeared walking parallel with the fence some ten meters in. Kane hunkered down in the shadows and waited for them to pass. Then he slipped through the gap in the fence, crossed the damp ground behind them, and slid into the trees on the other side.

Kane moved swiftly, sweeping left and right as he went. As he neared the edge of the tree line, the facility loomed large before him. It was a high-security complex with the minimum on the security front. There was no need for it. Every person held within the concrete walls was locked down securely in single cells that could only be opened from a central hub. Every guard within the compound had signed a document stating that they understood that should they be captured by any of the inmates, they would not be bartered for and should consider themselves dead.

Many considered those within consisted of the worst threats to America over the past few years. Homegrown terrorists, others from North Africa, the Middle East, Philippines, Indonesia, Iran, Afghanistan, Nigeria, and all countries in between that were thought to be threats.

And among them was an innocent woman who would be scared and confused.

Kane had made the decision that if it came to it, he would take no prisoners. It was a line he was pained to cross, but according to the intel given him by Alex Joseph, the guards were contractors, renowned for their brutality and shooting prisoners.

"Son," he'd said, "they're ruthless sons of bitches who were disowned by their mothers and disavowed by their country. They walk on the dark side, and to get this done, you'll need to make sure they stay there."

Kane's mouth stretched thin. He touched the cloned security card Joseph had given him. "It's good for twenty-four hours, son. After that, it will be reset. If you can't get in on the first go, you're screwed."

Kane had asked no questions about the acquisition, just put it in his pocket.

The Reaper sat on his heels, enveloped by the night, and waited. A few minutes later, the pop-pop sound of gunfire reached through the darkness from the east. Striker and Ruggles.

Kane waited for a further minute before moving.

Lights had come on, and guards were running toward the sound of the gunfire. Kane lifted his NVGs because they were flaring in the light.

He came off his heels and started forward. The Team Reaper commander crossed the open ground toward the complex and disappeared into the shadows.

A few minutes later, after the diversionary gunfire had ceased, more started—this time within the concrete walls.

INSIDE THE FACILITY

Two bodies lay in the sterile hallway, surrounded by an ever-increasing pool of blood. The two brought the tally to eight or nine. Spots of blood formed a trail along the polished concrete floor, some larger than others.

Empty brass 5.56 casings were scattered along the hallway, and like the blood trail, led to another dead man. This one wore a suit and tie. Two bullets had punched into his chest, dropping him where he'd stood.

The alarm was becoming annoying, like a nagging boil on the inside of a leg that rubbed with every stride. Kane did his best to block it out, but it was driving him nuts.

He raised the suppressed 416 and shot the shit out of the small megaphone speaker hanging from the ceiling. It stopped the immediate noise, but it was more than made up for in other parts of the complex.

Blood dripped from the tips of Kane's fingers on his left hand, courtesy of a bullet wound on his upper arm.

It wasn't life-threatening, but it was bleeding like a bastard.

Another shooter appeared ahead of him. Kane let the 416 go, and the strap it was attached to snapped taut as it took the weapon's weight. His right hand went to his thigh, and he pulled the P226.

The SIG roared and the man fell, his weapon spilling from his lifeless hand.

Kane pressed on.

The hallway turned right, and his path was blocked by a door. Opening it with the provided swipe card, he pushed through, surprised it worked.

On the other side was another hall almost identical to the one he'd just left. The difference was, this one had doors on either side.

As he walked down it, he peered into the rooms through the bulletproof glass that was set in each door at head height and measured half a foot square.

The first two were occupied by men in white jump-suits. The next held another man, this one in red. The fourth window Kane looked through framed a young woman dressed in a blue jumpsuit. Her long dark hair hung down her back.

She must have sensed him there because she turned to look at him, staring at his partially hidden face. When he saw hers, there was no mistaking that it was his sister. It was a face he'd stared at for hours every time he'd gone to see her, watching for a sign that she was about to wake from her coma.

Melanie's expression became confused, her head cocked to one side. Hurriedly, Kane used the card to unlock the door. It beeped at him but refused to budge. He tried again, and nothing happened.

"Shit! Shit! Shit!"

"The man," Melanie shouted at him. "The man in the suit."

Kane frowned. Then he ran back to where he'd shot his second-to-last victim. He checked the man's pockets and found a second keycard. This one was different from the other.

The Team Reaper commander ran back to the cells and tried it on Melanie's lock. It beeped, and he was able to open the door.

Kane stepped inside and reached out with his bloody hand. "Mel, come with me. Hurry."

"Who are you?" she asked.

Crap, she didn't recognize him.

"Mel, it's me. John."

"John?"

"Yes."

"Brother John?"

"Yes. Remember, we talked?"

She rushed forward quicker than he expected. "John! John, it's so good..."

Her voice trailed away. She stepped back. "You're hurt."

"Just a scratch."

"What's happening? Why are they doing this to me?"

"I'll explain later. You need to come with me."

"All right," she replied, her hesitation evident.

"Just stay behind me."

Kane raised his 416 and moved out into the hall-way. Melanie was behind him but not close enough. He said, "Put your left hand on my left shoulder and leave it there."

"John—"

"Do it, Mel."

He felt the pressure and started forward again. "Whatever happens, don't let go."

———

Something was wrong. Kane's and Melanie's passage out of the facility was going too easily. However, the sound of gunfire soon reached his ears, and he realized why. The others were engaged in battle with all the security personnel who were left.

Outside, Kane assessed the situation. He could see the flashes from the weapons on the west side of the compound. Striker and Ruggles had moved their position and looked to be heavily engaged. For a fleeting moment, he thought about joining them to help, but he was all too aware of the reason he was here in the first place. He turned away from the scene and said to Melanie, "Let's get out of here."

———

Striker was down but still in the fight. Ruggles, being his usual indestructible self, had his weapon on single-shot and was cursing every target he fired at.

"Get out of here, Senior," Striker called to him. "I'll cover your retreat."

"Fuck off," Ruggles growled. "No man left behind."

More bullets whipped around them as the security forces increased their rate of fire. Ruggles ducked and scooted over to Striker. "How's the wound?"

"Hurts."

"Pussy."

"Screw you," Striker shot back and replaced the empty magazine in his weapon. "Last mag, Senior."

"Yeah, me too. You figure he got out by now?"

"Maybe."

"Good." Ruggles threw the weapon on the ground. "Let's call it a night, son."

Striker nodded and threw his weapon beside his friend's. "All right, Senior."

They sat beside each other below cover and waited for the firing to stop. Ruggles said to Striker, "Let me take a look at that leg."

Six men loomed out of the shadows into the light. That was all that was left of the security force: six angry hotshots who figured to get them some payback for what had happened to their comrades. Their leader, a big man with a deep voice, said, "Say goodbye, assholes."

A fusillade of gunfire came in from the darkness, and the remaining security people died in a hail of bullets.

More figures emerged from the shadows, and a familiar voice said, "You two just can't help but get into the shit, can you?"

Striker stared at Borden Hunt. "Blame this old prick. He's the one."

"And here I was prepared to die at your side, son," Ruggles growled. "Not next time. I'll stand you up so they can get a better shot."

"You would, too," Striker opined.

"Rucker, get a look at his wound before he runs out of the good stuff. Did Reaper get away?"

"I sure hope so," Ruggles replied. "Or all this was

for nothing."

EPILOGUE

"WHAT IS IT?" Edison asked in a less than hospitable tone.

The voice on the other end of the phone said, "We've got a problem."

Edison listened quietly to the news, then grunted. "Get everything we have on it." He disconnected the call. Picking up another encrypted cell, he dialed a new number.

On the other end, President Richard Nelson said, "This better be good news."

"Not hardly. Kane got his sister out of the facility. Whoever was with him killed the security team before they left."

"Damn it, Brett. You were supposed to fix this. Where is he now?"

"We don't know."

"Shit. Put the bounty on his head. I want him found. Make it thirty million."

Edison's heart quickened with excitement. This was more like it. "Dead or alive, sir?"

"It won't make a difference, will it, with that amount of money involved?"

"Yes, sir, Mister President."

———

TWO HOURS LATER IN THE SKY OVER THE ATLANTIC.

One of the flight crew in the Globemaster walked toward Cara, holding a computer tablet and some earbuds. He held it out to her. "You need to see this."

She put the earbuds in and tapped the screen. What she saw was a press conference being given by Brett Edison.

"*...need to be on the lookout for these two people.*" The screen changed and showed a picture of Kane and his sister.

"*They are extremely dangerous and should be treated as such. They are responsible for the murders of several government officials and should not be approached. Instead, we urge anyone who sees them to inform the authorities right away. I reiterate, they are extremely dangerous, and we believe the pair are working for a foreign government. Therefore, I have been instructed by the President to issue a reward for their capture or information leading to their capture. That reward will be thirty million dollars.*"

Cara was stunned. "Oh, Reaper, what have you gotten yourself into?"

A LOOK AT: THE COLD HAND OF DEATH: A TEAM REAPER THRILLER

BY BRENT TOWNS

London is ablaze and the only ones who can stop it are the members of Team Reaper!

Three bombs have gone off in London, the work of Libyan Terrorists. Or is it?

MI5 brought in the team, now stationed in Hereford, to help investigate the bombings after the SAS were sidelined for an incident overseas. However, all is not what it seems as they soon discover, and Team Reaper is once again engaged in a life and death struggle from Libya to their adopted country's shores.

But an old enemy isn't finished with them and soon, Kane is drawn into a new game. One where winning means everything and losing is not an option.

AVAILABLE SEPTEMBER 2025

ABOUT THE AUTHOR

Brent Towns began writing in 2015 with *Last Stand in Sanctuary* and published his first hardcover Black Horse Western the following year. Since then, he's written many more westerns, action-adventure novels including the bestselling *Team Reaper* series, the novelization of *Bill Tilghman and the Outlaws*, and several *Commando Comics*. Based in Queensland, Australia, Brent writes late into the night.

If you're interested in sharing your thoughts in more detail, scan the QR code below! Your feedback is invaluable to him—and often helps shape his future writing endeavors.